BLOOD IN
ELECTRIC BLUE

Greg F. Gifune

FIRST EDITION PAPERBACK
ISBN 978-1-934546-11-6

DELIRIUM BOOKS
P.O. Box 338
North Webster, IN 46555
srstaley@deliriumbooks.com
www.deliriumbooks.com

Author Acknowledgements: Thanks to Rob Dunbar for reading this novel prior to publication, and for the subsequent conversations we had and the helpful and insightful suggestions he offered, all of which made the final draft of *Blood In Electric Blue* possible. Also, special thanks to Jonathan Whalley at *MiJon Technologies* who, when a virus hit my old laptop and was then unintentionally transferred to the only copy of this manuscript I had on disk, managed to rescue and save the original file of the novel from my badly damaged hard drive. Were it not for his expertise and diligence, *Blood In Electric Blue* (which was a little over half done at that point) surely would've been lost forever. And as always, thanks to my wife Carol, to Shane Staley and Delirium Books, and to you the reader.

For my mother and father.

"And sometimes, when I waken in a strange place, my memories of the journey that brought me there resemble, in fact, the vaguely incredible, often unbelievable memories of a dream."

— Patrick Roscoe
The Lost Oasis

PROLOGUE

The ocean looks different at night, more mysterious. Dangerous.

Despite the chill in the air, a blanket of fog rolls gently across the surface, the dark water in slow but steady motion, the tide rocking and gliding toward the promise of solid ground. A slight section of beach separates land from ocean. Beyond it and the growing fog, silhouettes of buildings and the vague twinkle of city lights peek through curtains of darkness.

Just beneath the waves, obscured by darkness and fog, something moves silently toward shore. Concealed in shadowy night water, it is neither fish nor man, yet moves with the grace and primitive power of a large shark, a creature slicing through the ocean with the confidence reserved for predators that have existed uncontested for millions of years.

Something similar to a human hand, the fingers long, clawed and webbed, breaches the surface and mistakenly brushes a large channel marker buoy, the last one between it and shore. The bell atop it clangs and echoes through the darkness, momentarily disrupting an otherwise eerily quiet night.

Blood In Electric Blue

As it moves closer to land the water grows shallow and its feet touch bottom, toes taking hold in the moist and murky sand. With a fluid and commanding motion, it stands, its body breaking the surface as it rises up to its full height, the arms and upper body dripping saltwater, the torso littered with seaweed and ocean debris.

There is little moonlight, but even in shadow it is apparent the being has undergone a metamorphosis, changing from sea creature to one better suited to land. Gone are the clawed and webbed hands and feet, the black eyes, the misshapen head, the flush ears, the tail and scales, the gills. All of it gone, replaced instead with human features.

As the being walks the rest of the way to the beach, it pulls the seaweed free and tosses it back into the ocean while wiping the debris from the rest of its nude body. It moves with a distinctly feminine and seductive gait. As it shakes its head, its hair falls free and cascades down along the now delicate and smooth shoulders, long wet strands dangling above full breasts barely visible in limited light.

It stops, considers its surroundings a moment, nose twitching, eyes staring, head cocked as it listens, hears, absorbs, the fog swirling, moving like smoke as it embraces the being. Not that hiding matters any longer. If anyone looks upon it now they will see nothing more than a nude, devastatingly attractive swimmer.

This is the place, it thinks. *She* thinks. This is the place I've searched for. He's here. Somewhere out there among the occasional lights but otherwise dark cityscape, the one she has come for is waiting, only now even remotely aware of what he is, what she is, of what is coming. Of what *has* come.

For him.

ONE

Huddled in the darkness of the studio apartment, staring at slivers of moonlight sprinkled along the baseboards and throughout the room as if placed there strategically, he dismisses his nightmare as it occurs to him that perhaps a definitive solution to the horror that has become their lives doesn't exist. He runs his hands across his head, finds remnants of hair matted and damp from perspiration, slick and clammy between his fingers despite the chill in the air. A burning sensation draws him to the pad on the middle finger of his left hand. It is scraped and raw, as it might appear had he spent the last few hours rubbing it against a rough surface. Extending his arms, he forces them into the path of moonlight. In contrast to the skinless circle at the tip of his finger, a pattern of cobalt veins traverse the pale skin along his arms, like netting.

Blood, in electric blue.

He next notices the thin gold bracelet on his right wrist and remembers a bar so many years before and a Haitian man named Roscoe, of all things, with a silver front tooth. Dignon bought the bracelet from a selection

Blood In Electric Blue

Roscoe carried in his briefcase. Less than a week later, Roscoe died in the alley behind the bar, what remained of his briefcase and those sparkling trinkets spilled about his collapsed form riding rainwater streams that trickled into nearby drainage grates. Dignon remembers him lying on glossy pavement, mouth open and caked with spittle.

The bathroom door opens and artificial light spills into the rest of the apartment, ruining the balance of moonbeams and darkness with the subtlety of a fist punched through sheetrock. "Who's there?"

Wilma trips her way into the room with theatrical flair and choreography that would have made Bob Fosse proud. Wearing only pantyhose, she appears typically harried and sullen both, a large white towel covering her chest, eyes decorated, face painted and powdered. "Who were you expecting," she asks, "Rosencrantz and Guildenstern?"

The toilet flushes and Barry emerges from the bathroom next, still fumbling with his zipper. "Hello, Dignon, didn't realize you were here."

Dignon acknowledges him with as little enthusiasm as possible.

Wilma switches on a lamp. "Christ, Dig, what is it with you and the dark? I could've broken my neck."

"There are worse things," Barry mumbles.

Wilma frowns as if mortally wounded; a hand pressed flat against the towel, neon pink fingernails holding it in place. "That's not funny."

"No," Barry says, moving to the kitchen. "It's not."

Dignon reaches for a bottle of beer hidden in the shadows along the floor next to him, raises it to his lips and takes a long swallow. Then he notices Wilma's hair, or lack thereof. He points at her with the bottle.

"What, love?" Her hands find the top of her head,

8

mascara-drenched eyelashes batting self-consciously. "Oh. Have you seen my blonde one?"

He motions to the row of Styrofoam heads draped in various colors and styles of wigs that line the top of the bookshelf on the other side of the apartment. "There, on the end, that's blonde."

"It's got to be the platinum one, Dig. Tonight's platinum night, I need—"

"Well put *something* on," Barry snaps.

"Why do you have to say it like that, with such a cruel edge?"

Barry takes a beer from the refrigerator, opens it and gulps some. "I say things exactly the way I mean them. It's called being genuine."

"I don't have time for this. I have to be at the club soon."

"Relax," Barry says through whiny, mocking laughter, "nobody cares."

"That's a—what a rotten thing to say."

"I just don't understand why you all feel the need to perform."

"Excuse me, did you say: 'you all'?"

"Don't get PC on me. You know what I mean."

"No, do tell."

"Is there some unwritten law, a chapter in the handbook that says all drag queens, transvestites and select transsexuals have to spend a certain number of hours onstage lip-syncing to Streisand and Garland tunes?" He looks to Dignon for validation but finds none. "By all means, be whoever you are, but just because you deck yourself out in sequins and put on heels and a wig doesn't mean you have *talent*, okay? Can we establish that once and for all, please?"

In a distant tone, as if she had suddenly thought of something else, she says, "I'm a waitress. I've never claimed to have any real talent, it's just for fun. Besides, I only perform when there's an unexpected spot, you know that."

"Perform. Christ."

"Well that's what it is, what am I supposed to call it?"

"Don't tempt me."

Wilma pretends to ignore him and moves across the room to the bookshelf. Inspecting the wigs, she sets one long fingernail in the crook at the side of her mouth and pouts more than necessary. "Stop being such an insufferable grump."

"You should never use a word like *insufferable*, Willie. It doesn't suit you."

"Okay. Stop being such a fucking grump. Does that suit me better?"

"It does, actually."

"Finally legit after all these years, praise the lord!"

"You know, sometimes you can be such a little..." Barry manages something smile-like and leans forward a bit, his beer bottle pointing the way, "Well, I'd say *cunt* but that'd be about as genuine as your singing."

Wilma spins back in his direction with the grace of a rabid figure skater. "At least I try. You just sit back in judgment like some grand poobah."

His smile fades. With his pointed features, curly-perm hair styled like an afro and his tall, pencil-thin frame draped in a shiny gray suit and open-collar black shirt, Barry looks like a refugee from a 1970's disco. Yet despite his rather comical appearance, he possesses an unmistakably violent edge. "Why don't you just quit while you're ahead, OK?"

"And I don't like you when you drink. You become, for lack of a better term, unpleasant." She turns to Dignon. "And *you*, you're not even supposed to be drinking with the medication you're on, are you?"

"I haven't been taking the depression pills, they're too strong."

"But I thought the doctor told you to—"

"They make me feel like a lunatic."

"Why do you let things torture you so? You're a good person, Dig, you're—"

"I'm a delivery man." Dignon finishes the beer and lobs the empty bottle across the room. It skips and bounces along the unmade bed. "And I'm not even *that* anymore."

"Guess I'll be changing the sheets tonight after all."

"Boring!" Barry downs the remainder of his beer, slaps the bottle onto the counter and grabs a long raincoat from the back of a nearby chair. "I'm out of here," he says, slipping into the coat.

"See you at the club?" Willie asks.

"Not tonight." He heads for the door, giving Dignon a casual salute as he passes. "See you later, Dig-man."

"Bye."

She follows him to the door. "Call me later?"

"We'll see," says Barry, and then he's gone.

Dignon waits a while before he asks, "What's your greatest fear, Willie?"

The question snaps her back into the present. She turns away from the door and concentrates again on the wigs. "Change, I guess. I'm a creature of habit."

"Mine's the exact opposite, the possibility that my life will never be any different than it is right now, right at this moment."

"You just asked me that so you could answer it yourself."

"You're a clever one."

"Stop being so gloomy, you've had a bad run that's all."

"A bad run? I'm forty-two-years-old."

Blood In Electric Blue

"That's impossible," she gasps. "That'd make me forty-four! Just look at me, I can't possibly be a day over twenty-five."

He doesn't laugh, though they both wish he had. "I don't want anything so special, I never really did. I just don't want...*this*."

"But then that's life in some ways, love. We want what we don't have. The fat girl wants to be thin and the thin girl wants to gain a few pounds. The girl with big titties wants smaller ones and the girl with little titties wants bigger ones. The blonde wants to be a brunette and the brunette wants to be blonde. And the redhead — *well* — let me tell you about red — "

"And sometimes people just want to be someone else entirely, right?" He struggles to his feet. "Sometimes they need to be something else, something — anything — other than what they are, than what they've convinced themselves to be." Dignon steadies himself against the wall with one hand and runs the other across the stubble along his cheeks and chin and throat. "Right?"

"Sometimes they do."

"Even if only for a little while."

"Yes, Dig, even if only for a little while."

He shuts his eyes, feels a tear pinch free and trickle the length of his face. It clings to his jawbone, dangles a moment then falls to darkness.

He's envious.

"Why are you crying, love?" she asks softly.

"Sometimes I feel like it's all coming apart, you know? Like I won't be able to hold things together much longer, I — like at any second it's all going to burst into pieces."

Somewhere outside a person shouts and a car horn blares.

"You live such an isolated life," Willie tells him. "You

need to get out there more, live a little."

"You live alone too."

"But I have more of a social calendar. Plus, I have Barry."

"Barry," he moans.

"Look, don't start, all right? Maybe if you got to know him better you'd —"

"He treats you like shit. If he ever lays a hand on you, I swear to God, I'll —"

"We're talking about you, not Barry. And he'd never do that. I'll put up with a lot, but not that. You know that." Willie scratches delicately at the corner of her mouth with a neon fingernail. "You've been through a lot," she says, "but you're not alone. You have me, and I love you."

"I love you too." Dignon looks at the floor awkwardly. "But you know what I mean."

"Yes, I do. I know what you mean. You were already having a hard time, and then that whole thing with Jackie Shine was just another log on the fire and —"

"I don't want to talk about that. Not tonight, OK?"

"I'm just saying, I know you've got a lot to deal with right now, but you're alive, Dig, you're alive. And as long as you're alive you've got a chance."

"At what?"

"Happiness, silly."

Neither speaks for a while.

Finally, Wilma asks, "What are you thinking about?"

Dignon doesn't bother to open his eyes, but can't be certain fear is the only culprit. "Roscoe, a man I once knew. He sold jewelry out of a briefcase. I didn't know him all that well, we frequented the same bar. One day, he died, had a massive heart attack and collapsed in the alley behind the bar. Except for a couple wakes here and there, I'd never seen a dead body before. His I saw by accident. I stepped out into the alley to relieve myself, and there he was. I remembered thinking, why is Roscoe laying on the ground? I thought he was drunk and had passed out back there. Then I looked into his eyes and I knew."

"How awful," Wilma whispers. "You never told me that story before."

"It was years ago, back when I was living in New York with Lisa. For some reason, I was remembering his body tonight, collapsed there in that alley. His face, and the way it looked, that dead stare, lifeless and stunned. Even in death he looked surprised, like he still couldn't believe what had happened to him. I think about him sometimes, and how when he got up that day, when he rolled out of bed and pulled his pants and socks and shoes on, when he brushed his teeth and took a shower and ate his breakfast, collected his merchandise into his briefcase and left the house, he had no idea what was waiting for him out there, that within a few hours it'd all be over and he'd be dead on filthy concrete. It was like that for Jackie Shine. It's like that for all of us, we just pretend it isn't." He opens his eyes, finds Wilma's pained expression. "I never thought I'd have to see anything like that again. I should've known better. It's like I'm some sort of death magnet."

"Don't say that."

"It's true, isn't it? I have been right from the start."

"Stop it, you're no such thing." Willie wraps her arms around herself, causing the towel to ride up her legs a bit. "You've got too much time on your hands to sit around and think about these morbid things. It's not healthy, Dig. Maybe you should go back to work and—"

"I'm never going back there."

"Then you need to start thinking about what to do with the rest of your life. Things can't stay like this forever."

He nods grimly. "I know."

Wilma comes close enough to wipe the remnants of tear from his cheek with her thumb. "It's going to be OK," she says through a gentle smile. "You'll see."

Dignon gives his brother a kiss on the cheek and quietly slips out the door.

TWO

Plumes of gray smoke cough from the factory stacks on the edge of town, deluging the dark sky as they tumble and turn in great giant spirals along the horizon. It's getting colder, and a steady breeze blows in off the choppy winter ocean, up over the coastline, slashing through town like a razor. It will snow soon. Dignon can feel it in the air. People always complain about the snow and ice, the cold, the winter, but then this is the northeast after all. He finds those complaints peculiar, if not wholly dishonest. How can people that have lived in these parts their entire lives complain about something so inherent to their location? It leaves him curious as to why they would live here at all. Unlike most, Dignon openly professes his love of snow, and has since he was a child. There's something magical about it, especially in the early morning or evening hours when it's dark and still and so quiet, and then suddenly, there it is, appearing from nowhere like an illusion. Otherworldly somehow, it's a transformation that takes place right before one's eyes, the mundane to the exquisite in an instant.

Greg F. Gifune

Though it's still a few weeks from Christmas, everything is draped in holiday decorations, lights and bows and synthetic cheer. Christmas carols, distorted and tinny through cheap speakers mounted on the telephone poles in the retail district play on an endless loop, and mammoth lengths of garland have been strung from one to the next, in silver and green and red. People move about, hurrying here or there, hustling and bustling, juggling packages, talking on cell phones, making plans, living their lives in frenzied bursts of rudimentary fear, ants scurrying through tunnels of sand, unable to stop, always on the clock, never looking back. And not one of them notices him. Not one returns his attempt at eye contact, not one offers a smile or even a sneer. More than disregarded, he is overlooked, and somehow that's worse. Yet there remains something oddly cathartic about being among other human beings.

Holding his paper bag close, Dignon pulls his coat in tight around him and continues on toward home.

There isn't a star in the sky. Later, when he remembers this, there will be.

Mrs. Rogo has decorated the front door of the building with a fake wreath, replete with red plastic holly and adorned with an imitation satin ribbon from which hang two small, slightly rusted jingle bells. She's also put up her imitation Christmas tree, which now blinks garish multicolor magnificence through the first floor window facing the street. On the steps the same ceramic three-foot-tall Santa Claus she's used for years stands beaming, one hand clutching a bell and the other a sack of gifts slung over his shoulder. Several spots on his coat are chipped, which results in white blotches across his otherwise red suit. It looks like he's been spattered with bird shit. The expression on his face reminds Dignon of the look his father often had when he and Willie were children, when he was so drunk he could no longer walk or talk, only sit collapsed with an imbecilic grin and those soulless eyes.

It's nearly seven.

Dignon lingers on the front steps long enough to better take in the neighborhood, the sights and subtle sounds, the feel of it all.

In the foyer, Bing Crosby holiday tunes seep from Mrs. Rogo's apartment, accompanied by the smell of roasting chicken. Dignon quietly takes the stairs to his second-floor digs, key at the ready so he can get inside before his landlord hears him. Much as he likes her, he can't deal with her tonight.

Once inside, he flicks the light switch. An overhead fixture comes to life, filling the area with a yellow tinted hue. His living quarters consist of one main room, an adjacent kitchenette and a small bath and bedroom in back. Modestly furnished and not particularly well kept, it has low ceilings, drab walls and ancient hardwood floors that have become scarred and worn over the years.

This is what I was hurrying back to? Looked more appealing in the dark, he thinks.

He tosses his keys on the kitchen table, grabs a beer from the fridge then flops down into a threadbare easy chair and fishes a used paperback from the bag he's been carrying. On his way home from Willie's he stopped at a local used bookstore he often patronizes, and after several minutes perusing the shelves, settled on *Mythical Beings in a Mortal World*. Though he normally sticks to novels, this bit of nonfiction looks interesting. Written by a professor, it is essentially a listing and breakdown of numerous mythical beings throughout human history, and their origins and influences on various cultures. It reminds him of the documentary television programs he watched as a child, like *In Search Of*, that covered such

Greg F. Gifune

topics as Bigfoot, UFOs, and the Loch Ness Monster. He's always found these kinds of things interesting and somewhat entertaining, so he suspects the book will serve as a pleasant distraction.

He glances around, realizes he's alone in the room. "Tibbs?"

A sleek black cat saunters from the bedroom, yellow eyes sleepy and squinting in the light.

"Got a new book, dude." Dignon holds it up. "Cool, huh?"

Not terribly impressed, Mr. Tibbs yawns, has a lengthy stretch then hops up on Dignon's lap and stares at him dully.

He pets Mr. Tibbs on the head then opens the front cover of the book and flips through the first few pages. He immediately feels an unsettling sense of foreboding and odd familiarity, but it weakens and leaves him almost as rapidly as it arrives. Published in 1980, there are numerous creases to the cover and some pages are faded and dog-eared, but otherwise it's still in fairly good shape. A deal at fifty cents, he thinks. In the upper left hand corner of the title page a previous owner has written in ballpoint pen: *This Book Belongs to Bree Harper.* A series of numbers follow. A phone number, he thinks, has to be. And oddly enough, a local exchange. Dignon has been a voracious reader his entire life, and most of his book purchases are of the used variety. Over the years he's come across numerous notes, names, addresses and phone numbers scribbled in books, there is certainly nothing unusual about that. But for some reason, this instance holds his attention. Bree. Strange name, he thinks, but pretty and lighthearted. It must be short for something. His mind conjures a vision of her, though he can't make out any specific features. *Hi, I'm Bree.* He pictures walking hand-in-hand with her down near the ocean on a starry night. This night even, once it begins to snow, the flakes fat and fluffy and turning in the sea breeze, mixing with the clouds made by their breath.

Wouldn't that be something?

Dignon tosses the book on a small table next to the chair. Mr. Tibbs kneads his lap a moment then carefully lies down. He begins to purr. Petting him with one hand, Dignon takes up the bottle of beer with the other and finishes it in a single, determined pull. The alcohol courses through him, but still, he can feel.

After some quiet time with Mr. Tibbs, just sitting and thinking, running his hands through the cat's soft fur and listening to the wonderful rhythm of his purr, watching the slow rise and fall of his chest with each breath drawn then expelled, and feeling the warmth pass from his underside into Dignon's lap, everything slows down. The world becomes hushed, like winter nights ought to be, as if in anticipation of something vaster that might otherwise be missed in the clamor of everyday life. In that softness, the stillness, he glimpses peace.

But by the time he realizes what it is, it's gone.

Some time later the beer runs out and Dignon switches to pot. It's not a problem. He's come to like marijuana, and sometimes it better suits his purpose.

It fails to stop the memories from returning however, and soon he is wandering about the small apartment like an errant pinball, bouncing from one corner to the next, a joint in one hand and the other motioning subconsciously, talking for him as monologues rage in his mind.

There is the job he held for so many years, the delivery position at *Tech Metropolis*, the largest electronics retailer in the area. There is the warehouse where he'd report each morning, meet up with the other two sets of drivers and delivery people to get their assignments for the day. There is Clarence, a six-foot-seven former high

Greg F. Gifune

school basketball star who runs the delivery department, a sullen and gangly man who wears nylon sweat suits and high-top Converse sneakers regardless of the weather, as if he might otherwise forget what an athletic prodigy he once was, and as if to alert the world that he is ready at any moment should the call come that will rescue him from the bench and return him to the limelight. But everyone, including Clarence – perhaps Clarence most of all – knows this will never happen. Knee and ankle injuries snuffed dreams of college and the NBA out long ago. Now he sits cramped in a small booth most of the day, a booth constructed almost entirely of Plexiglas, where he shuffles papers and fills out forms and barks orders at drivers and delivery people through his dispatch equipment. There are the other delivery teams: Outlaw and Boo, and Adam and Blondie. Outlaw is a biker type, a wannabe who rides on weekends and keeps his body rotund, his hair long, his beard unruly and his tattoos antisocial. He refuses to wear anything that doesn't have a *Harley-Davidson* logo on it. His partner Boo is a small Hispanic man with a shaved head and tiny, deep-set eyes. He is just over five feet in height, with a slight but sinewy build. He rarely speaks, but when he does it's in a muffled muttering style few can fully decipher other than Outlaw. Adam is a thirty-something African-American with a trim build. He is meticulously clean and tidy, and has the cleanest van in their small fleet. He keeps his hair closely cropped, wears freshly pressed shirts and sweaters and is often mistaken for a salesperson or perhaps a member of management rather than a deliveryman. Everyone knows he does this purposely because he plans to one day be one of the two. No one objects. The others hope he's right. His partner, Blondie, is the only female delivery person. A short and muscular woman with bad

Blood In Electric Blue

skin and a penchant for unfiltered Pall Mall cigarettes, her nickname comes from the short shock of peroxide blonde hair that looks as if it is exploding from her large, round head. In her twenties she was a professional wrestler on the independent circuit. Now nearing forty, she sticks to grappling boxes of electronics.

And then there is Dignon's partner. Jackie Shine looks like a poor man's James Dean, only about thirty years older than the original when he died. He wears barracuda jackets with the collars up, tight-fitting jeans and lots of hair gel, which he uses to keep his thick mop in place. There is almost always a toothpick in the corner of his mouth, and his eyes—squinty but expressive—are slightly askew, very sad but also somewhat primal, like a tiger that could turn on you at any second and tear you to shreds. Jackie Shine walks with an obvious limp, an uneven gate that nearly comes off as a short hop because his right leg is a prosthetic limb. He has had this since he was nineteen, when, in the jungles of Vietnam, he stepped on a landmine and his real leg was taken from him, blown away just below the groin. Jackie Shine is a drug addict and an alcoholic. He eats prescription painkillers like some pop breath mints, and drinks whiskey continuously, either from a flask he keeps tucked in his coat pocket, or after work at bars, restaurants, his apartment, anywhere he can.

None of them started out to work there. None fantasized of one day delivering TVs and stereos, computers and office furniture. They have all arrived by accident, refugees from other places, other dreams. And though it is honest work, it is hard and not terribly rewarding work, the hours long, the pay average, the shifts tedious.

While Dignon has worked there for years, Jackie Shine is really the only person he works with he truly counts as a friend. The others are acquaintances, people he sometimes goes and has a drink with after work, or exchanges small talk with first thing in the morning. They are people he does not know in any meaningful context, and yet for so long, other than for Willie and Mr. Tibbs, they are all Dignon has.

On what becomes the last day he will ever work there, Dignon arrives as usual, meets up with the others in the warehouse and waits for their assignments. The driver is the one that goes to Clarence's little glass booth for the itinerary, and since Jackie Shine always drives, Dignon waits over by the enormous mountain of items ready for delivery, brought forward by a forklift from the stock areas to the loading dock on big wooden pallets. Once they have their shipping list and destination addresses, the teams will load the items into their vans and be on their way. He holds a Styrofoam cup of coffee in each hand, one for himself, one for Jackie Shine, feels the warmth bleed through to his palms and fingers as he watches his partner, Outlaw and Adam standing in single file before Clarence's booth like unruly children summoned to the principal's office.

None of them have any idea what will happen in just a few short hours.

Dignon has seen many things over the years as a delivery person. Rarely like bad porno movies suggest, scantily clad women answering the door and such, but rather things far more disturbing. He once set up a large screen television and a surround-sound system in a rundown tenement while in the next room a handful of heavily armed drug dealers readied their goods for distribution. The leader, an enormous man with a gun on each hip and bands of bullets draped across his chest like a villain in an old western, had handed him a five hundred dollar cash tip, motioned to the table where numerous drugs and guns were scattered and said,

Blood In Electric Blue

"Forget it all." Dignon nodded and took the money while Jackie Shine waited outside in the van, smoking cigarettes and taking sips of whiskey from his flask. Why the men had spent the money on such expensive equipment in a building they were so obviously only using for a day or two, Dignon never knew. In his business, you learned not to question. You did your job and left. And he always "forgot it all." Except for one delivery, when he and Jackie Shine had brought video equipment to an address in one of the worst sections of town, only to find an older man, perhaps sixty, well groomed and dressed in an expensive suit and tie there to greet them. After he had shown them where to drop the equipment he had thrown tips at both men and quickly ushered them out. But he and Jackie Shine had seen the room with only a mattress and tripods set up, the room with plastic bags of children's clothing and toys thrown about. They had seen the children seated at a long table in another room, having a lavish dinner and laughing, another well-dressed man at the head of that table. These were clearly poor children, neglected children few wanted or would miss. The oldest was perhaps twelve.

Once outside, Jackie Shine stopped and looked back.

"There's nothing good happening in there," Dignon had said.

"Yeah," Jackie Shine agreed. "No shit."

"We better tell the cops."

"I don't like cops."

"We have to tell somebody."

Jackie Shine had two children somewhere on the west coast, both grown by then. He might've been a grandfather. He took a pull from his flask, watched the building a while longer then stuffed the booze back into his coat. "It won't do any good. You see the suits on those two cats? Money, that's what that was. What the hell you

24

think men like that are doing in that dump? Didn't you see the look on the face of the one that answered the door? He look worried to you about a couple delivery guys? They got enough money to do whatever they want. Probably already got everybody paid off to leave them alone anyway. They blow into town, do their thing and are gone within a few days, on to the next place before anybody even notices."

"But that's the whole point. We did notice."

"You call the cops if you want. I'm blind as a bat, brother man. Last drop of the day, I'm going home."

Dignon held his ground. "They're little kids, we have to do something."

"Then make the call, hero." He headed for the van. "Just leave me out of it. They want statements and all that, tell them I waited in the truck the whole time."

"Why? What do you care about protecting scum like that?"

"I don't protect nobody," he said. "I keep my head down and I drive my van."

Dignon felt rage rising in him, not so much at his partner but at the men in the building. Destroyers, he'd thought, that's what they are. "Then I'll do it."

Once a few blocks away, Dignon had him pull over. He ran to a payphone and anonymously dropped a dime.

Neither heard another thing about it. Maybe the cops did something, maybe not. They'd never know, though Dignon had checked the newspaper and television news reports for weeks afterward, hoping to see a story regarding a child pornography ring that had been uncovered and broken up.

No such story ever surfaced.

"What'd I tell you?" Jackie Shine said several weeks later. "Long as the right hands get the right amount of cash, nobody gives a shit about anything."

Blood In Electric Blue

"Somebody should do something, for Christ's sake."

"We could go back to my place, get some firepower and go pay them a visit. Up for a little frontier justice? Want to go *Taxi Driver* on their asses?" Jackie Shine nodded. "Yeah, I didn't think so. Just like war, long as somebody else gets to do the dirty work, it's all about freedom and what's 'necessary.' Long as it ain't their asses on the ground doing the killing and dying."

"You know I didn't mean it like that."

"Just making a point. Besides," he said softly, "I won't never kill another living thing ever again, I don't care what it's done." He gave Dignon a pat on the shoulder. "Don't worry about it, kid. They're probably long gone anyway."

"That's not the point. Those kids, they—"

"Shit, in 'Nam I saw things done to children that made molestation seem merciful." He flinched, as he often had when speaking of his time at war. "After a while you just learn to say fuck it, you know? Don't mean anything anyway."

"It means *something*," Dignon said. "It has to."

"That's the lie they tell us. But the truth is, Hell exists, and it's right here on Earth. I've seen it. Now there may be a good Lord and there may be a Heaven too, but until we get there, we're on our own down here. There's no right or wrong, never was, never will be. There's just the shit we do and the shit we don't do, what we can stomach, what we can't and how much we'll take either way. Look at me. Think anybody gives a shit I lost my leg—my fucking *leg*, man? I was nineteen-mother-fucking-years-old, should've been getting stoned and banging every girl that stood still long enough. Instead I get to be facedown in a puddle of mud and blood and teeth and hair with strings and bone and shit dangling where my leg used to be. All that death and madness, for what—tell me, man—for what? For a bunch of fat rich old white men somewhere, that's what. They ring the bell and we run the maze. They get fatter and richer and people like me, if we're lucky, we get lighter, leave an arm or a leg or maybe even both behind. If not, we go crazy or die. And after all the TV reports and all the speeches, all the Senate hearings and all the talk and crying and medal ceremonies and movies and books and stupid-ass T-shirts and tribute concerts and all the rest of the horse-shit civilized people do to convince themselves they *do* care stops, it all just goes back to the way it was. You think I got it bad, brother man? Swing by a vet's hospital. Better yet, ask ten people on the street where one is. Tell the poor bastards in there anybody gives a shit. Go ahead, I dare you. Tell them their lives and their 'sacrifice' meant something. Hand out some bumper stickers or have a bake sale, that'll make their fucking day. Nobody cares, man. Not about them, not about you, not about me, not about those kids."

"Well that was uplifting, you depressing fuck."

Jackie Shine laughed. It was something he rarely did, which is perhaps why Dignon remembers it so vividly whenever he thinks of him.

He also remembers his partner was right. They both moved on with their lives. Neither pushed the issue with the children and strange men in that tenement. They tried to forget about it, hoped for the best, and felt ashamed for having done so.

Life, such as it was, rolled on.

"They try to sell us on killing, but they're lying," Jackie Shine would often say. "Once you kill something—I don't care what it is, a man, a deer, whatever—something changes in you. Most times you don't even realize it at first. But it's in there, in you, something that wasn't there before. And you can't ever get rid of it. If you're smart, you do your time in this life, you mind your business, you don't fuck with The Man and you lay low. Maybe, if you smoke plenty of good dope, drink lots of hard liquor and crank one out every morning in the shower, you make it through the day without losing your mind, or worse. But even then, sooner or later something gets every single one of us. The trick is, don't be afraid. Never go out afraid, kid. Don't give them the fucking satisfaction."

On the last day they worked together, they were on their final delivery and only moments from the end of their shift. The last drop was a stereo system and DVD player being delivered to a duplex in a working-class neighborhood.

Dignon remembered Jackie Shine had been in a hurry to finish up. His flask was empty, the last of his whiskey had run out and he was anxious to call it a day and get to the liquor store.

While Dignon unloaded the boxes from the back of the van, Jackie Shine took his clipboard and paperwork to the front door and knocked. After several attempts and no answer, he stepped back and looked up at the second floor. A window slowly slid open and a middle-aged man poked his head out.

"*Tech Metropolis*," Jackie Shine called to him. "Got a delivery for this address."

The man glared down at them suspiciously, shook his head no and waved an arm at them as if to shoo them away.

Dignon stopped unloading. "Sure you got the right address?"

"Yeah," he said, glancing at his clipboard and comparing the numbers to those on the building. "This is it. Must be for somebody besides this douche, maybe someone else lives here too, who knows?"

"Can you come down and open the door, sir?" Dignon called.

The man again waved them off.

"Like I got time for this bullshit," Jackie Shine muttered. "Hey, listen up, buddy. We got a delivery for this address, OK? Now you either open the door and we bring it in for you, or we leave it here on the street, got it?"

The man shrugged.

"I don't think he speaks English," Dignon said.

"Fuck him then, leave it on the street."

"We can't do that, it's against policy." Dignon moved closer to the building. "Can you open the door, sir?"

Jackie Shine reached for his flask then remembered it was empty. He hobbled over to the van, threw the clipboard onto the dash then pulled his wallet out of his back pocket and let it hang open, the way a police officer might show a badge. "Watch this, bet this gets his ass down here." He approached the door and pounded on it again, then held his wallet up and aimed it at the man. "Open the door! Do it now! Immigration, asshole! Open up!"

"Jesus," Dignon sighed. He returned to the van, prepared to put the items back and leave. "Come on, we'll try again tomorrow."

"Immigration! Open the door, now!"

The man's face fell, and he disappeared back into the building.

Dignon leaned against the van, wiped perspiration from his brow. It was a particularly hot summer day, the humidity off the charts. Sweat dripped from every pore, and he remembers just wanting to go home and sit in front of the oscillating fan in his den.

Jackie Shine put his wallet away and chuckled. "Told you that'd get him moving. We'll do the drop and be out of here before you can say green card."

But when the front door opened, the man began to scream at them. Dignon saw right away that he was holding something, and at first, he remembers he thought it was a broom or some sort of stick. But as the clearly terrified man stepped farther into the light, he realized what it was.

Jackie Shine turned in time to see it too.

"Fuck," he said quietly.

And then a deafening boom filled the air. There was smoke, Dignon remembers smoke wafting about. Not a lot, just a small patch of it. And he remembers Jackie Shine leaving his feet, his arms out on either side of him as his body vaulted backwards and into the air in a spray of blood. It all happened so quickly, yet he remembers it more in slow-motion, like a dramatic death scene in a movie.

Dignon stood frozen, staring at the man in disbelief.

He continued to scream things Dignon couldn't understand.

He remembers looking down at Jackie Shine. He was already dead, a toothpick still stuck in the corner of his mouth. And the blood, he remembers that most of all. There was so much it didn't seem possible it all could've come from one man.

"Don't," Dignon said, or perhaps only thought, he still can't be sure all these months later.

The man pulled the trigger, but this time it made only a clicking sound.

And then the man seemed to see Jackie Shine for the first time. Realizing what he'd done, he dropped the shotgun to the floor then followed it, collapsing into a sitting position in the doorway, face in his hands as he wept uncontrollably.

Dignon sat next to Jackie Shine. He could feel

warmth emanating from the jagged hole where his chest and stomach had been, the insides now his outsides. There would be no melodramatic last words or goodbyes.

At that moment Dignon went numb.

In shock, he had no idea what to do, so he simply took one of Jackie Shine's hands in his own and held it tight.

Later, after the police and the paramedics and the hospital and the reporters and the representatives from the company, after all the chaos in the subsequent hours and days following the event, Dignon learned that the delivery had been for the man's son, who had not been home at the time. The man had a history of mental illness and aggressive behavior, spoke not a word of English and had apparently believed the men in the van had come to deport him.

All Dignon knew was that Jackie Shine was dead. He'd survived the horrors of Vietnam to come home years later and die in the street like a piece of trash.

He doesn't understand any of it. But then, he never has.

So Dignon staggers about his tiny apartment, joint in hand, and replays the scenario again and again.

From his position on the couch, Mr. Tibbs watches like an attentive parent.

Dignon has not returned to work since that day. Thankfully the insurance through the company provides for a disability payment, and since his doctor has officially deemed him disabled due to "severe psychological and emotional distress as a result of post traumatic stress disorder" he is able to collect his monthly stipend and continue to live at the near-poverty level he has become accustomed to for so long.

He thinks of his mother just then, and his pacing

Blood In Electric Blue

comes to an abrupt halt. He wants so desperately to see her face at that moment, the one he's seen in a photograph. But it eludes him. *She* eludes him, lost in shadow and night. He sways, nearly falls over but catches himself as he comes to rest near a window overlooking the street.

Dignon squints, tries to focus on the beam of light coming from the streetlamp on the far side of the street. He watches it a moment, and in that patch of artificial light, sees what look like countless tiny dust motes coursing through the night air.

It has begun to snow.

THREE

It is still early morning when Dignon awakens, but in winter it's hard to differentiate this time of day from the middle of the night. He lies in bed and watches patterns of shadow play along the ceiling. There are degrees within the darkness here, each level unique. He studies them a while, tries his best to decipher their mysteries. As always, Mr. Tibbs is by his side, snuggled up close, warm and purring softly. The neighborhood, the building, it's all still asleep. He imagines Mrs. Rogo in bed in the apartment beneath him, wrapped in leopard print blankets and imitation satin comforters, her little wiener dog Schnitzel curled up at the foot of the bed. Of course Dignon has never actually seen Mrs. Rogo's bedroom, but in the silence of his own isolation, he envisions it quite vividly. He wonders what she dreams about, this former go-go dancer who looks like some aging porno star or stripper, her hair teased too high, her makeup too heavy, her clothing too dated and better suited to a younger woman, this late-fifties widow who has never been anything but kind to him and Mr. Tibbs. Guilt rises, and he feels badly for having snuck into the building the night before. She was undoubtedly sitting at her kitchen table with a roasted chicken and all the fixings, a bottle of champagne chilling, candles burning, old Christmas tunes blaring, waiting for people who will never come or perhaps no longer exist. He often wonders why she still makes such elaborate meals for herself. She has a daughter who seldom visits, and several grandchildren. Dignon has only met Mrs. Rogo's daughter twice in all the years he's lived there. He doesn't care for her. She's as plain and uptight as her mother is garish and glitzy, a harried and unpleasant woman who barks at her children and rolls her eyes whenever Mrs. Rogo says anything. Yes, he thinks, he should've gone and seen her last night, even if only to stop in and say hello, to let her know someone cares. They could've at least shared a nice meal together. And Mr. Tibbs is always welcome in her apartment as well; he and Schnitzel get along famously. But instead there he was, just feet away occupying the space above her head, drinking and slowly killing himself the same way his father had so many years before.

No, not exactly like his father, he thinks. He's nothing like his father, yet they share at least one of the same demons, perhaps more.

The cat raises his head and looks back at him, as if he'd heard Dignon thinking. He yawns, reveals a flash of impressive teeth then stands, climbs up onto Dignon's chest and sits down.

"Hungry?" The cat stares at him with an expression that illustrates this should already be evident. "OK, pal, come on."

As Mr. Tibbs hops down to the floor, Dignon rolls out of bed, rubs the back of his aching neck and consults the alarm clock on the nightstand. The digital display reads: 5:38.

Greg F. Gifune

After a detour to the bathroom, where he pees, swallows a few extra strength Excedrin and splashes a bit of water on his face, Dignon shuffles to the kitchen area, pours some dry food into the cat's dish, refills his water bowl then checks the refrigerator. A carton of milk, some orange juice, a small tin of coffee, a half-eaten brick of cheddar cheese and something in Tupperware he thinks was at one point Mexican food, occupy the top shelf. A few condiments sit in the trays on the door. Otherwise, the refrigerator is empty.

He grabs the coffee, scoops some into the coffeemaker then turns it on and goes into the den to wait while it brews. He sits in his chair, in the dark, and looks to the window. It won't be light for a while yet, but he can see it has stopped snowing.

Dignon rubs his eyes, draws a deep breath and hopes the headache crawling into the back of his skull will go away soon. He feels weightless there in his chair, flimsy and hollow, like everything of substance has escaped him while he slept, leaving him little more than a husk, an emptied shell tottering about by rote.

Perhaps mistakenly, he looks to the book on the small table to his right.

He switches on a lamp, picks up the book and flips it open. A quick paragraph or two about some exotic mythical being should sufficiently fill the time until the coffee is finished. The pool of light washes over him dully. He looks to the lamp, a basic cream-colored plastic number with an off-white shade he purchased years ago at a discount store. He makes a mental note to pick up a package of stronger bulbs next time he's out.

Leaning closer to the patch of light, Dignon turns to the title page, and again, the writings in ballpoint pen catch his eye. *This book belongs to Bree Harper.* He hesitates. His finger is tucked behind the corner of the page, but he doesn't turn it. Instead, he reads the phone number a few times, focuses on the name and realizes he has begun to nervously gnaw his bottom lip.

Who are you? He wonders. The book itself is from 1980, but there's no way to date the information written in pen. At some point this Bree Harper, or some subsequent owner, turned the book in at the used shop for something else, another book or a store credit. That could've occurred years or only days ago, it's impossible to know without asking one of the clerks, and Dignon would never do that. Even if he wanted to, how would he explain his need to know? What difference would it make when they received the book, and with the volume of used books they take in each week, would they even remember a single paperback like this? Doubtful.

His finger slowly moves across her name then slides down to the phone number. He tries to imagine what she might be like. Where does she live? What does she do? Is she married? Does she have children, grandchildren even? Does she have a boyfriend, a girlfriend? Is she alone? Is she young or old or somewhere in between?

Is she happy?

What if she's alone like he is? What if she's waiting for something too, anything that might save her, rescue her from this life? All these people missing one another, Dignon thinks, runaway kites floating just beyond reach.

He wonders if he's seen Bree Harper before without even knowing it. Maybe he's seen her in the used bookstore or in one of the shops around town. Maybe she's passed right by him. Maybe—

A gust of wind rocks the building and the window facing the street creaks. He hears the furnace in the basement kick on and the old radiator against the wall begins to rattle and hum. In the kitchen, the coffeemaker gurgles.

Greg F. Gifune

Lisa comes to him then, like she does so often in early morning. It makes sense, he supposes, that he thinks of his parents when he's drunk and of Lisa in the quiet moments of the mornings after. Her memory pushes his fantasies of Bree Harper aside, proving that even after all this time it's still impossible for him to imagine love without remembering her. The time he spent with Lisa was the best year of his life, after all.

He remembers her face, the feel of her skin, the texture and smell of her hair, and the way her body felt against his. Even all these years later he can recall her with startling clarity. Or maybe he's fooling himself. Maybe he's dealt with her in memory and shadow for so long that what he perceives as reminiscence is in actuality blurred fantasy, empty spaces conveniently filled in and smoothed over like pottery taking shape on an ever-turning wheel, the end result never quite realized, the glob of clay and water an unfinished vision of what might have been.

Yet he knew when Lisa left him he'd never recover. He'd felt it even then.

"You're leaving?" he'd asked.

She nodded, her things collected into a small suitcase at her feet. "I don't want this anymore, Dig."

"You mean you don't want me."

Silence.

"There's someone else, isn't there?"

"Does it matter?"

"Of course it matters."

"Then yes, there is."

"Why?" he'd asked, angry at himself for allowing the emotion to get the better of him when he'd tried so desperately to prevent it. "What did I do?"

"Nothing, it's me."

"What did *you* do then?"

Blood In Electric Blue

"I fell out of love with you," she said softly, "and I'm sorry."

"How do you fall out of love? It doesn't seem fair that you know how to do that and I don't."

"It's not."

He has not seen or spoken to Lisa since.

Twenty years. Twenty *years*. He was only twenty-two at the time. It hardly seems possible it could've happened so long ago. Most days it's like a piece of some entirely separate life. In a way, maybe it is. Nothing has ever felt quite that real since. There were a few girlfriends here and there, negligible relationships that lasted weeks, sometimes even a few months, but never anything like he had with Lisa. It's been more than a decade since he's been in a relationship, and though he stopped trying long ago, the idea of a relationship of value is still something he thinks about. But he hasn't even been on a date in nearly five years. He can't remember the last time he had sex. Jackie Shine used to encourage him to go with him to a prostitute he'd seen regularly, but Dignon always declined. He cannot imagine anything less erotic than paying a woman to pretend she desires him. Even this horrible loneliness is preferable.

If nothing else, it's real.

And here I am, he thinks, forty-two. It seems he just turned thirty not so long ago, and now his thirties are over. He may not yet be old, but his youth has left him in the flutter of an eyelid. He wonders if one day he'll find himself sitting in this chair thinking the same of his forties, his fifties, perhaps even his sixties and seventies, should he live that long, his entire life a slow burn, a fatigued look back over his shoulder at...at what?

This book belongs to Bree Harper.

Ignoring his headache, Dignon pushes himself to his

feet and returns to the kitchenette. He digs the phone-book from a drawer next to the sink, drops it onto the counter and turns the pages until he reaches *H*. Quickly sliding a finger down the columns, he locates listings for Harper. There are several, but only one has a local exchange: Sabrina Harper. His fingertip lingers on the name, presses down into the sheer paper. Sabrina. Sah-bree-nah. Bree.

The phone number matches.

With a rush of excitement he reads the address listed: 36 Borges Lane. Over the years, he has delivered to virtually every part of the city. A map appears in his head, and he locks on Borges Lane, a small side street a block or two from the ocean and not far from the retail district.

The aroma of freshly-brewed coffee fills the air. Dignon puts the book aside, fixes himself a mug then goes through the mail on the kitchen table. Junk flyers, a light bill, and his monthly disability check. Though the amount of compensation is the same each month, he checks it anyway, then wanders back to the den and stands before the window overlooking the street. He watches the sky a while, numerous scenarios and possibilities forming in his mind.

* * *

After a shower Dignon puts a Band-Aid on his damaged fingertip, dresses and tells Mr. Tibbs he'll be back soon. The cat hops up on the chair and faces the door, watching him with a look that says he'll be on guard until Dignon returns.

It is a cold, raw morning. The huge factory stacks along the horizon pump their usual endless clouds of mystery into an otherwise clear gray sky, but what he notices first is how busy the sidewalks and streets are for

Blood In Electric Blue

this time of morning. During the holidays everything comes awake earlier, things become more congested and electric. Ironically, despite the masses, he never feels quite as isolated as he does during the Christmas season. Everywhere he goes he's faced with images of family and children, love and romance, togetherness and peace, brightly-wrapped packages, carols, Santa Claus and magic and all things happy and wonderful, all of which serve to remind him just how empty his life has become. As if he needed to be reminded of such things. Still, despite it all, particularly during this time of year, Dignon struggles against allowing his soul to be swallowed by despair and grief. He views Christmas and the holiday season in general as an enigmatic but fascinating possibility, an elusive but attainable state of being. Like Shangri-La, though remote, should he have any hope of finding it, he must believe in its inherent existence and never stop hunting for its promise of paradise.

Time passes quickly, and his mind wanders as he walks. When it clears and he refocuses, he finds himself in a familiar neighborhood. He stops, looks to the building where Jackie Shine lived. Dignon searches for the street sign and other markers to make certain he has, in fact, walked this far in what seems such a short time. The apartment is in an old house, a former single residence converted to apartments several years ago and out of place with the rest of the architecture on the street. He wonders if someone else lives in Jackie Shine's apartment now. He had few possessions. Dignon has no idea what became of them. All he knows is that the body was cremated and the remains flown to California where his children reside.

There is no trace, no remnant of Jackie Shine's existence here. One day, Dignon thinks, when everyone is gone, there will be nothing left but buildings like this one. Buildings and machines and all the things Man has constructed and left behind. No people, no animals, just things, and no one to remember or care about any of it.

Dignon hurries across the street and down the block toward the retail district. The smell of eggs and bacon and sausage leaks from a diner on the corner and fills the air. His stomach rumbles with hunger, and he stops long enough to peer through the front window at the giant grill and two chubby men in white outfits and paper hats wielding spatulas. He continues on, down the street to the outdoor mall. Again, he hears the Christmas music blaring from tinny speakers, and notices the garland strung along the poles, which looks decidedly different in the light of day, even more unnatural and peculiar. As he stops, he pushes his hands into his coat pockets to warm them and surveys the stores.

Within the hordes of people, Dignon mostly notices other men. There seems to be a disproportionate number of them shopping for Christmas gifts for their significant others. But there are also lots of couples buying toys and gifts for their children. He people-watches a while and wonders what it might be like to have a life like that, a life with someone to share it, someone to love, with a family. Dignon likes children, always has, but has never seriously thought about having a child of his own. The delicate nature of children frightens him, and he knows firsthand just how fragile they can be.

He notices several men coming and going from the *Victoria's Secret* a few doors down, most carrying large handle bags with the smiling face of a model wearing a Santa cap emblazoned on the side. He moves closer, studies the window displays then ventures inside.

An intense combination of images slams into him the moment he moves through the door. He hesitates and glances around. Tables are positioned throughout the

Blood In Electric Blue

space, filled high with stacks of various items of clothing and lingerie. Directly in front of him is a bone-white, headless, armless female torso that looks like it's growing up out of one display table. Adorned in a red lacy bra, it is surrounded by a sea of neatly positioned, identical bras in an assortment of colors. Dignon stares at the mannequin — or whatever it is — uncertain if the feeling slinking through him is one of vague lust or something more akin to creepiness. There is something at once sinister and darkly humorous about this dismembered chunk of imitation human being that leaves him mesmerized, albeit briefly.

"Can I help you, sir?"

A young woman to his right seemingly materializes out of thin, though heavily perfumed air. Her ample breasts jut out at him from beneath a white sweater to form an abnormal shelf in the middle of her chest. She is otherwise astonishingly thin, which makes her head and bust appear large and awkward in comparison to the rest of her body. An inch or two taller than he is, which makes her about five-ten or eleven, she has angular features that match her bony physique and razor-straight black hair that hangs like glossy curtains on either side of her face, framing beady eyes, a long nose and a mouth made fuller with the application of maroon lipstick. She raises a spindly arm and jangles a series of gold bracelets on her wrist, smoothing one side of her hair away from her face to get a better look at him while also making sure he has seen the diamond sparkling on her ring finger.

"Hi," Dignon says.

The clerk raises a drawn-on eyebrow. "Yes?"

"Yes?"

"Can I help you?" she says again, this time phrasing it as if she suspects he may not fully comprehend English.

"Sorry, I..." He realizes he has not thought this through. He has no idea what he's doing here. Dignon looks around as if trying to remember what he'd come looking for. "I need a Christmas gift."

"OK." The woman holds her hands down in front of her, one clasped over the wrist of the other. "Are you looking for anything in particular?"

Frantically scanning the store, he settles on a stack of plush bathrobes on a table to his far right. "A robe," he says, pointing, "one of those, actually."

She seems to come alive, and strides over to the table. He follows, trying to anticipate her next question. "Full-length or mid-thigh?" she asks.

Unsure, he looks to the robes. "Uh..."

"Who is the robe for?"

Dignon makes eye contact with her, notices in her expression she has already assumed it must be for his mother or sister. "My *wife*," he says defiantly. "And I think she'd prefer full-length. Yes, definitely full-length."

Without bothering to hide her surprise, the saleswoman says, "OK, did you want a particular color?"

"Red, I—she likes red."

"Size?"

"Medium should do it."

"They're really nice," she says, almost kindly. She removes a folded red robe from the pile and holds it out with both hands, presenting it to him like an award. "I have one myself, I just love it. I'm sure your wife will too."

"Yes, she likes robes, she—she likes them very much."

"Super."

At the counter he tries to appear unfazed by the fifty-dollar price of the robe. Although it's well beyond what he can afford, he hands her the cash like he makes these kinds of purchases all the time. The woman places the robe and a folded box for it into a large carry bag, the same one he saw so many other men carrying. "Thank you," she says blandly, handing the bag across the counter to him. "Have a happy holiday."

"You too, thank you." He offers a quick smile. She doesn't return the gesture.

Once outside in the sobering cold air, he decides he'll give the robe to Willie as a Christmas gift. It should fit her and she'll love it. But for now, he holds the bag proudly, hoping others will see it and consider him just another guy out shopping for his wife. It feels good to play this game for once, to at least pretend he is not the odd-man-out. He walks briskly, swinging the bag back and forth as he goes, careful to cross the street and move a bit more discreetly as he approaches his old stomping ground and passes *Tech Metropolis.*

By the time he reaches the outskirts of the retail district the exhilaration passes and he again begins to think about Bree Harper.

The smells and sound of the ocean grow closer as he cuts across a short avenue and onto Borges Lane, a rather drab, residential working-class street. Even as he walks the narrow lane, casually glancing at the building numbers, he silently scolds himself. What are you doing here? What the hell is wrong with you? Are you some sort of stalker now? None of this is a sign. It has no meaning whatsoever. She's just some woman who innocently jotted her name and phone number in a book you happened to pick up, stop obsessing.

Willie's right, he thinks. He simply has too much time on his hands, and it's not healthy. When he was working he had neither the time nor the energy to obsess about things. Now he has nothing *but* time, and it's more difficult to control his fixations. Perhaps it's his recent focus on the past—his childhood, his parents, Lisa and all the rest—that has led him here, to this stranger. Regardless of whom she may, or may not be, the fantasy of Bree Harper is a preferable distraction.

The dialogue in his head stops.

#36 looms before him, an unimaginative six-story apartment building the color of faded paper, a dreary rectangle standing on end with tiny symmetrical, square, socket-like windows carved into its face.

With the conspicuous *Victoria's Secret* bag at his side dashing any hope of subtlety, Dignon slows his pace but keeps moving, watching the apartments through the twisting clouds of mist his breath forms in the cold air.

The building stares back with its black eyes.

There's no way to tell how many units there are, but he notices a small foyer just inside a set of double glass doors at the front of the building. Beyond them, he can make out what appears to be a series of small mailboxes built into the wall on the far side of the foyer. There's no doorman, and he sees no security equipment, cameras and the like. He can't be certain, but it appears access to the foyer is more than likely possible without the use of a key, though there does appear to be a buzzer system.

Dignon heads for home, a plan already taking shape in his mind.

FOUR

There are only two mirrors here. One is in the bathroom above the sink and acts as the front panel to his medicine cabinet. The other is a full-length model that hangs on the back of his bedroom door. Dignon often forgets about that one, as he rarely closes the bedroom door for fear he may catch a glimpse of himself passing by. But on this morning, after returning from his robe shopping adventure and his reconnaissance mission to Bree Harper's apartment building, Dignon takes his copy of *Mythical Beings in a Mortal World*, slips into his bedroom and shuts the door behind him. He isn't exactly certain why he does this, but the need for increased privacy seems necessary. As the door closes however, he fails to turn away in time, and looks directly into his own eyes.

This is not what Dignon sees in his mind when he imagines himself visually. His is a dated version, a younger, thinner, healthier and more vibrant one. This is someone else. This is what's left.

He wants to turn away but for some reason cannot.

There he is, dumpy and balding and haggard, a pathetic look on his face, a silly book clutched in his hands and an even sillier idea running through his head.

Greg F. Gifune

Who is this person?

Rather than answer, Dignon leaves the image behind and slowly walks to the bed. He sits on the edge, the book in hand and the telephone on his nightstand just inches away. He rehearses his lines again, lips moving silently, then flips the book open to the number, grabs the phone and makes the call. There is an empty sound on the line, a pause in time as his finger hovers above the final digit that will complete the connection. He feels a tremor move through him. The moment it passes he stabs the button and the call goes through.

It rings once…twice…three times…

Hang up, he tells himself. Just hang up, this is crazy, it's—

"Hey, it's Bree," a female voice suddenly answers. "I'm either out or I can't get to the phone right now so please leave a message after the beep and I'll call you back first chance I get."

Dignon hangs up before the tone sounds and the recording begins. He looks to the alarm clock. She must be working, he tells himself. Of course, she—most people have jobs you stupid bastard—she must be at work. He assures himself he'll try again later, but for now he sits on the bed replaying the sound of Bree Harper's voice in his head. She sounds as intelligent as she does kind. Her voice is light and pleasant, sweet but articulate. The memory of it makes him swoon like a heartsick character in some cheesy romance novel.

What is wrong with you? Why are you—

Stop, he thinks. My God, *stop*, what—what the hell do you think you're doing?

Dignon stands, paces. Relax, it's OK. It's all right. Call her back later.

His body calms, the muscles slowly relax and the tension slips free. But his heart continues to race with the

Blood In Electric Blue

fervor of a teenage boy who has just called a girl for the first time to ask her out on a date. Beneath the Band-Aid, his raw fingertip pulses in time with the beat of his heart. It's been a long time since Dignon has felt this alive.

He again catches himself in the mirror then angrily pulls open the door and slams it back into the wall with a hollow thud.

Mr. Tibbs sits just outside the doorway, staring at him quizzically.

"Sorry," Dignon says.

The cat sighs.

"I called, Tibbs, I actually did it. She wasn't home."

Mr. Tibbs slowly shuts his eyes and then just as slowly reopens them.

Dean Martin Christmas tunes begin playing downstairs in Mrs. Rogo's apartment, reminding Dignon that he has not yet put up his Christmas tree. He wasn't sure he was going to this year, but suddenly feels it might be a good idea after all.

He goes to the closet in the hallway, Mr. Tibbs trailing, and from the top shelf pulls down a white plastic bag closed with a drawstring. Inside is the tree. Well, not exactly a *tree*, more a bush, really. He opens the bag and pulls it free, a squat artificial number he bought a few years prior and has used every year since, about one-foot high with little white lights built directly into its artificial branches that automatically blink once it's plugged in. He stares at the small tree, the extent of his holiday decorations.

"Merry, merry, joy, joy," he mutters.

Once in the main room, he makes room on a small table near the window, sits the tree down and plugs it in. The white lights twinkle and come to life. Mr. Tibbs hops up onto the table, sniffs the branches then looks to Dignon, pleased with this latest development. As the cat curls up next to the tree and gazes out the window, Dignon returns to the closet, finds a roll of wrapping paper left over from last year, and wraps the bathrobe. His skills in this area are, at best, adequate, and the end result is a passable, though unorthodox-looking package.

He recalls the salesclerk speaking to him as if he were a moron. *Can I help you?* Is it so awful, so unthinkably outside protocol to simply say hello? Is common courtesy such a stretch? What right does she have to act as if he doesn't exist as a fully realized human being?

Maybe it's hard for her too, he tells himself. She probably has to fend off men hitting on her all day, or rude customers causing trouble. Maybe her cynicism, if that's what it was, is justified. Who knows what she's been through? His resentment softens, but sometimes Dignon wishes people like her could see the decency in him. Why is he always made to feel like a troll periodically emerging from beneath bridges to unintentionally frighten small children? Who are these people to make him feel this way when he's never done anything to warrant such treatment? Is he supposed to stand in the street and scream, "I'm a good person!" in order to convince them?

He wonders if Bree Harper will behave that way toward him when they meet, if she'll dismiss him as some partial entity, an insignificant blip on her radar.

Dignon hopes not. For now, that's all he can do.

Soon, he'll know for sure.

*   *   *

There is time to kill, and hours to burn. With *Mythical Beings in a Mortal World* in hand, Dignon sits in his easy chair and opens the book to the first entry.

Blood In Electric Blue

~BANSHEES~
Believed to be elf-like beings, Banshees are heard but rarely seen. Creatures of the night, their infamous wailing, which is known as "keening," is primarily found in legends from Ireland, Scotland and Wales. It is believed that when one hears the cry of a Banshee outside one's home, the death of a family member or close friend is imminent.

He imagines such beings living here, concealed in darkness while crying proclamations of looming catastrophe, their wails dismissed or mistaken for other, more easily explained sounds. Wouldn't it be something if they really existed? Would he or anyone in this godforsaken place notice even if they did?

He closes the book, and in his mind, attempts to conjure a vision of what a Banshee might look like. But instead he is met by the flood of thoughts already residing there, thoughts that surge through his brain like rapids in wilderness. An endless dialogue, the constant chatter ricochets about, searching for avenues of escape. Or maybe it doesn't want out at all. Maybe *he* wants to purge himself of this affliction, but the thoughts are quite content to remain where they are, endlessly rattling about in his head. If only they'd quiet down for just a while, he could get his mind some rest. But that is just a fantasy now. True rest; be it physical, psychological or emotional is a ghost.

He tries to remember what he was like before.

Before. Before what? Did *before* ever truly exist?

Dignon looks at his watch. The second hand slowly sweeps past the six, climbs toward the nine. There is something ominous and unsettling about this, but he can't quite figure out what.

The air-breaks on a nearby public bus hiss loudly and cause him to focus on all that is happening just beyond his windows and door. Downstairs, Mrs. Rogo has switched to Frank Sinatra. *I'll Be Home for Christmas* creeps up through the floor as lights twinkle on the Christmas bush. *I'll be home for Christmas*, sings Sinatra, *if only in my dreams.*

Dignon remembers his father playing this song on the old record player in the den during Christmases while he and Willie were growing up. Their father would sit in a chair with a drink in one hand and a cigarette in the other, tears streaming down his cheeks while never uttering a word. Once, when Dignon and Willie were still little boys, Willie had asked their father why he was crying. The response was a backhand full in the mouth. Dignon can still hear that sound, that awful crack his father's hand made when it connected with Willie's teeth. He can still see his brother's head snap back, and the blood running from his lips and gums while Christmas songs played and pretty lights sparkled.

"It's your fault," his father said that day, glaring at Dignon with disgust. "You did this to me. You did this to him. You did this to all of us. You."

The song ends. Another begins a few seconds later.

Dignon stands, tosses the book aside. He trembles in the shadow of those memories, hands clenched into fists. Sometimes he wishes he could set it all straight, fix everything he's ever broken, take back every lie he's ever told, heal every wound he's ever inflicted, intentional or otherwise. He wants to be clean. He wants to be innocent.

Mr. Tibbs looks back over his shoulder at him. A sympathetic glint flashes in the cat's eyes before he turns back to the window and the theater just beyond the glass. His is an uncanny ability to absorb the world free of stipulation, and in quiet moments, when they sit together and Mr. Tibbs gazes at him adoringly, Dignon is witness to an unconditional love he can never achieve himself.

Blood In Electric Blue

Though he loves the cat dearly, he can only hope to one day love him with the same categorical purity with which Mr. Tibbs loves him.

The cat begins to purr.

Following his lead, Dignon breathes slowly, steadily, and eventually the tension lessens. His hands unfurl, release, and the trembling ceases. But even now he has no idea what to do with himself, because it is not horror, not all that is ugly and evil and grotesque and sorrowful that overwhelms and paralyzes him. It's the beauty, the heart-wrenching, magnificent beauty of the world and everything in it, the constancy of it even in dire circumstances and amidst the worst conditions, that leaves him weak, troubled and insignificant.

He joins Mr. Tibbs at the window. As Dignon pets him, the cat purrs louder but continues to look through the window, all that is happening out there infinitely more intriguing to him than anything within these walls. Dignon considers the street below, and hopes for the same. It is a sheer curtain, this partition separating here from there, and yet, huddled in his little space with his best friend, the outside world seems distant and alien, a universe away.

Banshees, he thinks, laughing lightly while watching the human zoo. Or maybe we're the Banshees, Dignon reasons. You and I, Tibbs, apart from the rest, crying out warnings no one notices, and not because they can't hear our wailing, but because they choose not to.

Nikki, a woman who lives next door, emerges from her building and stands on the front steps looking around as if gauging the direction of the wind. Her usual pitch-black clothing matches the spiked, multicolored hair that decorates her head. She wears boots with enormous padded platforms that look like something from a '70's glam band, carries a huge black purse with a skull and crossbones on it, and sports several facial piercings. Rings adorn every finger of both hands, and though she is covered in winter wear and a thick black duster, Dignon has seen her in summer and knows she has multiple tattoos on her arms, legs and back. Her makeup consists of black lipstick and black liner and shadow that give the effect of spiders nesting around her big, expressive eyes. All of it serves to make her pale skin appear even more so. In her early thirties, she strikes him as too old to still be going with this look, and though her style is deliberate and carefully calculated, Dignon has always thought she was cool and avant-garde in a way he wishes he could be too. He doesn't know her well, but in the few years she has lived in the neighborhood, Nikki has always been nice to him. She says hello, offers a smile and, despite her ghoulish appearance, usually has something pleasant to say nearly every time they pass each other on the street. She dates both men and women — mostly musicians and artists from their looks — but never the same one too long. She works at one of the more exotic clubs over by Willie's apartment, a place he has never been to but has walked by numerous times. He's not sure exactly what it is she does there. As he watches her it occurs to him that he doesn't even know her last name. In fact, the only reason he knows her first name is because Mrs. Rogo once mentioned it to him. Otherwise she would simply be that woman next door. Dignon wonders if that's how she thinks of him too, as that guy next door. If she thinks of him at all, that is.

He watches as she finally descends the steps, marveling at how she can maneuver in those boots at all. Her clomping gait in these monstrosities is oddly fascinating, unintentionally comical and inconsistent with Nikki's otherwise rough and self-possessed appearance.

A pair of men in suits and dress coats hustle past,

undoubtedly on their way to some business meeting or sales pitch. They slow their manic pace long enough to snicker at Nikki. One of the men points at her boots and barks out a mean and nasty laugh so loud Dignon can actually hear it through the window.

Nikki scrunches her face up and flips them the finger as she safely reaches the sidewalk. The men laugh and give each other congratulatory jostles as they continue on their way, proud of their effortless malice.

He feels no connection or kinship to people like that whatsoever, and for this he is grateful. They might as well be lampposts.

Then again, maybe he's a hypocrite. No, he tells himself, I'm nothing like those guys. The boots *are* funny, but they don't grant me permission to hurt or ridicule her. They're just boots, what difference does it make what she wears or how she —

Nikki trips as she crosses under his window, topples from the high boots to the sidewalk. She throws her hands out in front of her to break her fall, but she drops awkwardly, and her shoulder hits the edge of the curb. As her purse falls free and skids off along pavement, she rolls through the remainder of the fall, flops into a puddle and finally comes to rest on her back in the gutter.

As a handful of passersby stop to help her, one man suddenly turns and looks up at the building, staring directly at the second-floor window, as if whoever stands behind it is to blame.

Dignon backs away, out of sight.

*   *   *

He cannot remember precisely how long he has sat staring at the phone, but it's been quite a while. Things have changed, the day is different. He can feel it. The sky is grayer now, the clouds heavier, which diminishes the light through the windows and casts the apartment in a dull hue. Even the air he breathes feels altered. There's been a shift in…something.

The radiator against the wall rattles as the basement furnace comes to life. He imagines that ancient ogre squatting, dirty and rusted in the dark cellar below him, a freakish relic leftover from a bygone era. The cellar in this building has always made him uneasy. There's something creepy about it, with its cement walls, low ceiling, dank odors, and dark corners. There is nothing new down there, only banished things tucked away and forgotten. It is a place no one goes to unless they have to. He remembers the cellar in their home growing up, and a knot quickly tightens in the pit of his stomach. Dignon rubs his eyes until the memories recede. When his vision clears, he again focuses on the telephone, as if willing it to dial the number on its own.

Could he possess that kind of power without even knowing it? He wonders. Did he somehow cause poor Nikki to fall in the street? Was it his fault? Did he subconsciously will it into reality? He didn't want her to trip, he'd simply worried about her trying to walk in those boots.

Visions of the two men in suits crossing a busy street flash in his head. A car slams into them both, sending one into the air and up over the hood before he crashes through the windshield. The other is pinned beneath the front tires, mangled and screaming in bloody agony.

Heart racing, Dignon blinks rapidly until it all leaves him. Suddenly his flesh turns clammy and cold. Like death, or something close.

A current of fear arcs through him. Could he be having a heart attack? He seems to remember reading somewhere that people often become gray and clammy before or during heart attacks. He forces a nervous swallow, stands and places a hand against his chest. His heart thumps against his palm. He feels no chest pain or pressure, no aches in his shoulders or pains shooting down his arm, just the fierce pounding. Is he sick? Maybe that's it, he's sick and — *cancer,* could he — could he have cancer? Maybe something inside him is sick, an organ or something. Maybe whatever it is has stopped functioning properly and has become diseased. A tumor, he could have a tumor somewhere and not even realize it.

On cue, a dull ache pulses across his abdomen.

Years ago, before he'd quit smoking cigarettes, this would've been a perfect time to light up. After a few drags he'd feel better, and yet, he thinks, maybe it's all those cigarettes he smoked back then that are making him sick now. Maybe it's the dope he now sometimes smokes instead. Maybe it's given him cancer that's growing inside him, spreading and slowly rotting him from the inside out. Maybe it's in his brain and that's why he can't think clearly lately. He envisions black tissue inside him, his lungs and intestines dark and decomposed, sees flashes of him vomiting and soiling himself with blood and feces.

He closes his eyes against the surging panic.

Dignon begins to pray. *"Hail Mary, full of grace, the Lord is with thee. Blessed art thou among women and blessed is the fruit of thy womb, Jesus. Holy Mary, mother of God, pray for us sinners now, and at the hour of our death. Amen.*

After a few moments, the fear leaves him.

"Thank you," he says softly. Though Dignon is a lapsed Catholic and not a terribly religious person, he has prayed to the Virgin Mary since he was a little boy. He has always felt close to her. A small ceramic statue of her he's had since he was a boy still adorns his bureau, wrapped in a set of rosary beads that once belonged to his mother. It often gives him comfort, but he chooses his prayers to the Holy Mother judiciously, calling upon her only when he feels in desperate need of her divine intervention. She has never let him down, never ignored him, and this time is no exception.

He sits back on the edge of the bed. "What the hell is wrong with me?" he asks the floor. The carpet in here needs to be cleaned, he thinks. Maybe Wilma was right. Maybe he should never have gone off the depression pills. Or maybe he needs something even stronger. Maybe it's not a physical affliction he needs to worry about at all, but a mental one. He turns, forces himself to look at the mirror on the back of the bedroom door.

Could I be crazy? Would I know if I was? Could I tell?

"How fucking cliché is that?" he sees himself ask. Dignon turns away from his reflection. Pick up the phone. Just pick it up. Do it now. "I can do this," he says. He grabs the phone and dials before he can change his mind.

It rings twice, and then: "Hello?"

It's her. He recognizes that beautiful voice.

"Hello?" she says again, this time with uncertainty.

"Yes—uh—hello," he says, clearing his throat. "Is Bree Harper there?"

"Speaking."

"Hi." Follow the lines you practiced. Stay calm and follow the lines.

"Who's calling, please?" She sounds a bit annoyed.

"I'm sorry to bother you, but—"

"Look, if you're selling something, I'm really not interested, OK? It's cool, I know you have a job to do and you're just trying to earn a living, but—"

"No, it's nothing like that." Dignon hesitates a

Blood In Electric Blue

moment. He can hear her breathing. "Actually, uh, my name's Dignon Malloy, and I was over at the Main Street Park here in town earlier and happened to find a book that had your name and phone number in it. It was on a bench and it looked like maybe it had been left there by mistake, I wasn't sure—it's only a paperback—but I thought it might be something you'd want returned or…"

"It had my name in it?"

"Yes, ma'am," he says, adding the "ma'am" out of habit from talking to customers for so many years. "I just—I don't mean to bother you—I just thought maybe you'd lost it, and, I like books myself, and I know I've lost some before and would've liked to have them returned, so I just wanted to call and let you know I'd found it and…"

Please say something, he thinks. Please.

"What was the book?"

He tells her.

"Oh, I remember that one. Wow, it's so nice of you to call…I'm sorry, what was your name again?"

"Dignon."

"Interesting, is that a family name?"

The question catches him off-guard. She speaks to him like they're old friends. "Yes."

"Well, listen, thanks for the taking the time to call, that's so sweet."

He tightens his grip on the phone. "No problem."

"Strange thing is I know I didn't lose it in the park because I never bring books with me to the park. But obviously I misplaced it at some point and it ended up there somehow."

He is relieved she's forgotten she turned it in at the used bookstore. Or maybe she didn't. Maybe she really did lose the book somewhere and someone else turned it

58

in.

"I would like to get that one back, actually," she says. "It's a fascinating book."

He nods even though she can't see him. "If you want to give me your address I can drop it in the mail to you, or, I'm going downtown in a little while—"

"Oh, you're right in town too?"

"Yeah, I—if you're going to be anywhere near the downtown area later I'd be happy to bring it to you." She remains silent for several seconds. "We could meet somewhere public," he adds.

"You're sure it's no trouble?"

"No trouble at all."

"I sure would appreciate it, that's awfully nice of you."

"I'll be downtown in about an hour, is that OK?"

"Sure, that's fine. Why don't we meet at *Jerry's*, the coffee shop on Main? Does that work for you?"

"I'll be there," Dignon says through a smile he cannot prevent.

"How will I know you?"

"I'll be the guy near the door holding the book."

She laughs. It is the most contagious and amazing sound he's ever heard.

"OK, easy enough!" she says. "See you in an hour. And thanks again."

"You're welcome."

"OK, bye."

"Bye."

She hangs up. Dignon listens to the dead air for several seconds, unable to believe he's actually pulled this off. The nervousness is gone, replaced with a surprising glee he has not felt in years. He finally returns the phone to the cradle. In an hour he'll be standing right in front of her. Bree Harper.

Blood In Electric Blue

It seemed almost too easy, he thinks.
It's destiny. It has to be.

FIVE

Dignon moves quickly down the front steps of his building, the wrapped present under one arm and Bree Harper's book beneath the other. A chilly breeze blows in off the ocean. The weather reports called for the possibility of more snow this evening. The last batch of late-night flurries left no accumulation, but meteorologists believe this next front will be more substantial. He gazes out at the giant stacks coughing smoke along the horizon. They never stop, day or night, continually blanketing the skyline like everlasting storm clouds. Someone should do something about that, he thinks.

As he crosses toward the street, Dignon notices a small bloodstain along the sidewalk near the curb, a slashing smear of it where Nikki fell earlier. He looks back at her apartment as if expecting to find her there in her big boots offering an "I'm OK" wave. Instead, in the front window of his own building, Mrs. Rogo's Christmas tree suddenly comes to life, distracting him. It's still a bit early for lights, it won't be dark for another hour, but Mrs. Rogo more than likely has another elaborate meal planned and will be tied up in her kitchen preparing it until long after nightfall.

Blood In Electric Blue

After a brisk walk of perhaps fifteen minutes, Dignon reaches Wilma's neighborhood. Predominantly commercially-zoned, it is a four-block area literally on the outskirts of town, the last section of city before forest, and eventually, state highway takes over. This has not happened by accident, but is rather a carefully calculated and long executed move by the powers that be to keep the kinds of things offered in this area in a single, segregated district. There is a change that occurs when one crosses from other neighborhoods to this one, a shifting of sight and sound and even smell. The buildings and streets are not quite as well-kept or well-lit, yet things are considerably more vivid here than in the rest of this otherwise bland and unimaginative little city. Still, many people avoid this section of town, some even fear it. Dignon, however, doesn't feel uneasy here at all. Not because he frequents any of the clubs or shops, but because Wilma has lived here for eons and is known in the neighborhood. By extension, most regulars of these streets know who Dignon is as well, or at a minimum knows his connection to Wilma.

Her apartment is above a pool hall in a building sandwiched between a strip club and a small art-house movie theater. The drag bar where Wilma works as a waitress and part-time performer is a few blocks down, near the end of an alley. There are usually a lot more people on the street, but it's still early and the cold is probably keeping many away or indoors. Most of the neon lights and flamboyant signage has not yet been activated, which gives the neighborhood a peculiar look reminiscent of a carnival sleeping in daylight.

The smell of pizza from a parlor across the street drifts through the air.

His stomach rumbles, he hasn't eaten in some time, but music thumping from inside the strip club draws his attention from the aroma. A young white guy with dreadlocks hangs near the door, arms folded across his chest. He smiles at Dignon conspiratorially. "It's cold outside but it's nice and warm inside. Can you dig it?"

"No," he says without slowing his stride. Where do they find these fucking people? He ducks into the doorway leading to Wilma's second-floor apartment, and quickly climbs the long staircase. The space is cramped and dark, like a tomb. It's always made him uncomfortable, the walls and ceiling so close, battered with nicks and abrasions scarring the dark wood. It reminds him of a motorcycle show his father took him and Willie to when they were children. One of the attractions was a giant wooden barrel-like contraption with open steel stairs that led to a matching balcony surrounding the top lip of the structure. Beyond the railing, patrons could look down inside the barrel and see three motorcycle stunt riders literally riding around inside the walls, defying gravity with speed and often coming within inches of one another during their performance. Mesmerized, Dignon watched with mouth agape. At seven, it was to that point in his life the most amazing thing he'd ever witnessed. When the show was over, the main rider, a scruffy man decked out in leathers like his partners, held his helmet up and explained that much of their income was derived through donations. He asked those who had just seen the show to toss money down into the barrel, and as part of his appeal, asked everyone to notice the countless scrapes and nicks in the wood all around him. As he pointed out many of them, he explained each of those notches signified a false move by riders over the years. Each gash was a reminder of a maimed or even killed rider. That's how dangerous this work was, he told them, and much of the donated monies would go to those fallen "heroic" riders and their families. Dignon remembers staring down at the marred wood and wondering who these people were who had died or been horribly crippled inside this contraption. He and Willie both threw a quarter down, aiming for the man's helmet. His last memory was of that man catching coins in his helmet and thanking everyone while reminding them the next show would take place just ten minutes from then.

As Dignon climbs the stairs he takes in the various gashes in the wood around him, curious as to what they might be reminders of.

After three locks disengage, Wilma swings open the door and lets Dignon in. "Hey, love. Don't you look dapper?" She puts a hand to her face as he passes. "And *someone* smells positively scrumptious."

Since the other day, Wilma has put up a tall Christmas tree in the corner. It is not yet decorated, but a few boxes of previously stored decorations are stacked neatly near the base.

Dressed in an imitation silk robe and furry slippers with three-inch heels, Willie closes the door and saunters in after him. Her makeup is only partially done, but her wig for the evening, a short red model, has already been fitted and styled. "Just got the tree this morning, isn't it fabulous? Dominic over at the pizza place helped me pick it out before he opened. He carried it up here all by himself, poor baby. Thank God for chiseled Italians. Of course when the girls heard I was going tree shopping with Dominic they all rolled their sloppy asses out of bed and joined the festivities. You should've seen it, a bunch of bleary-eyed queens gathered around sipping coffee and drooling while poor Dominic hustled that tree up the stairs. Barry was supposed to come with us but he was called away on business. What else is new, right?" She looks to the tree and smiles. "Isn't it gorgeous? Kind of nice after all those years of Charlie Brown trees I've had, no? A bunch of the girls are coming over tonight after work, we're going to get hideously drunk and decorate it. You should come."

"I will if I can." Dignon holds out the package. "I can't stay long, just wanted to drop this off for you."

Momentarily speechless, she takes the box from his hands. "You didn't have to worry about getting me a Christmas present, Dig. I know things are hard right now."

He shrugs. "It's just a little something I thought you'd like."

"Of course I'll like it. I'll love it. What is it? Can I open it now?"

"No."

"Do you honestly expect me to wait until Christmas morning?"

"Yes."

"How unspeakably cruel, I hate you."

Dignon laughs, goes to a chair near her dressing table and sits down.

She follows him, leans in and kisses the top of his head. "Thank you, Dig."

"Merry Christmas."

Wilma carries the present to a table by the tree and sets it down. "So are you going to tell me why you're all dressed up and wearing cologne?"

"I'm not dressed up."

"Honey, I haven't seen you in anything but jeans, sweatshirts and sneakers in more than a year. For you, this is opera gear, OK?"

Dignon looks self-consciously at the khaki pants, loafers, pullover sweater and pea coat he's wearing. "I have to meet somebody later and I wanted to look—I don't know—I guess I wanted to look...you know...nice."

Blood In Electric Blue

She stops and cocks her head. "Oh my God, do you — say it isn't so — Dignon, do you have a *date*?"

He shakes his head. "Don't start, OK? It's not a date, exactly."

"Well what *exactly* is it then?"

"I have to return a book to someone." He holds it up as evidence.

Wilma licks her lips. "Who is she? Tell me all about it."

"Nothing, it's —"

"Details, damn it, I need details." She scampers into the chair at her dressing table, crosses her legs and drops her hands into her lap. "Tell me everything."

"Willie, there's nothing to tell."

She frowns. "Never leave your sister twisting in the wind, love."

"It's just a woman I met," he says, trying to find some version of things that will satisfy her and allow them to talk about something else. "I have this book and it belongs to her and I'm meeting her at a coffee shop downtown so I can return it. That's all."

"That's more than enough if you play your cards right, baby." She laughs, swings back toward the mirror over her dressing table and the huge Marlene Dietrich poster on the wall behind it. After selecting a brush she begins to apply a maroon lipstick. With her free hand she hits the remote for her stereo and fills the apartment with Gloria Gaynor. "So, who is she?" she says over the blasting music. "Where does she come from? Who does she hope to be? When do I get to meet her?"

Dignon gets up, goes to the bathroom and closes the door behind him.

"Dig, I was only playing, for fuck's sake!"

He leans back against the door and draws a deep breath. The room is small, and the lone window faces the brick side of the building next door and provides a blurred view of an alley through the mottled glass. On the wall is a little framed photograph of his brother from long ago. It is the only evidence in Wilma's entire apartment that William once existed. In the photograph he is no more than ten or eleven, his hair a mop of full brown locks, his eyes big and bright. He seems so impossibly small and young, such a delicate and handsome boy. Dignon can barely remember this version of Wilma, but the longer he looks into his eyes, the clearer the memories become. Willie holds a plastic kickball, and sitting next to him is Homer, the cat they had as children. Behind them is a glimpse of shrubbery and the house they grew up in. This photograph has been in Wilma's bathroom for years, it's been there all along, Dignon has just never taken particular notice of it. Now he cannot stop noticing it. Willie seems unusually happy in the photograph, but Dignon doesn't remember being present when this picture was taken, and can only assume it was their father who took it, though that seems an unlikely thing for him to have done.

Dignon reaches out, touches the past.

The glass is cool, lifeless as the little boy behind it. This child is long dead. But his was a griefless death in many ways, as he'd really been Dignon's sister all along. William simply did not survive their childhood. Wilma did. His brother reinvented and reborn as his sister, she has been alive now for so long it's difficult to remember her any other way. Still, this is who she is, who she always was, really, deep in her soul. No amount of pain was able to destroy that, and the intrinsic beauty of this leaves Dignon weak and reeling. He's suddenly teetering between all out panic and an odd sort of acceptance that nothing can save him from the overwhelming emotion pinning him down and strangling him, crushing him into oblivion, dust.

Daddy, don't. Please, Daddy, don't.

He snatches his hand away and falls against the wall. Screams tear through his head. All those years ago, could the Banshees have been warning him even then, gathered outside that dreary old house?

Dignon goes to the sink, runs the water a moment and splashes a bit on his face. It sobers him, brings him back. He flushes the toilet purely for effect then ventures back out into the apartment.

Wilma is there to greet him in a tight, black, sleeveless dress. "Shirley MacLaine," she says, striking a seductive pose. "Sweet Charity. What do you think? Did I nail it or did I nail it?"

He nods. "You nailed it. You look good."

"Good as in..."

"Good as in beautiful."

She smiles coyly. "I was only teasing before. I didn't mean to upset you."

"What about me, Willie? How do *I* look?"

She pads over to him in stocking feet and gives him a pseudo hug so as not to muss her hair, dress or makeup. "Adorable."

"No, seriously, do I look all right?"

"Yes!" She waves her hands around dramatically. "You look stellar, all right? Honey, you're a good-looking man, you just don't realize it. You've also got a very sensitive soul. Women love that in a man, trust me."

A spiteful laugh escapes him. "Yeah, all the chicks dig me. If my balding head and beer gut doesn't get them I've still got my man-tits and fat ass to dazzle them with. And if that doesn't do it I can always fall back on my sensitivity."

"Why do you insist on degrading yourself like that?"

"It's what I know."

"You're just afraid." She moves away, back toward the dressing table. "You're the same frightened little boy you were when we were children."

"We were never children."

"Yes we were." Snatching up the remote, she silences the stereo. She notices his bandaged finger but looks away. "Once," she says, quietly now, "for a little while."

"I don't remember."

"Do you know why?"

"Do *you*?"

She answers by squeezing shut her eyes. "Stop, OK? Just...stop."

Dignon bows his head, ashamed at having hurt her. Again. "I'm sorry."

Recharged by his apology, Wilma puts the remote aside and goes to her closet for a pair of shoes. He envies her resiliency, her ability to flip a switch and wrap herself in a protective cloak that at once shuts out the darkness. "OK, this is what I know," Wilma says. "You never got over Lisa. You haven't even tried since then, not really, and that was twenty goddamn years ago, which for some, is a lifetime." She finds a pair of black pumps and turns back to him, the heels dangling from her fingers. "You've never loved anyone but her. You've never allowed yourself to. You shut down because the first serious relationship you ever had—in your late teens and early twenties no less—didn't work out. Well, welcome to the dance, Cha Cha, most romances don't last, especially first ones. Most chew us up, spit us out and rip our hearts apart. They make us old before our time, OK? But what else is there? What is there besides love, instead of love? It's all we've got, sweetheart. It's all there is."

"You're wrong," Dignon tells her, voice shaking. "I've loved a lot of women. I fall in love all the time. Sometimes I feel so much love I don't know what the hell

Blood In Electric Blue

to do with it. I've got nothing *but* love, Willie. Thing is, somewhere along the line somebody's got to love you back."

Wilma watches him, eyes dark.

"Lisa wasn't the only woman I ever loved," he says. "She's the only woman that ever loved me."

Silence follows as Wilma steps into her pumps and straightens her dress. Finally, after what appears to be much thought she manages a response. "To quote the great Helen Hayes: 'There is only one terminal dignity — love.' What else is there to say, Dig?"

"I have to go."

Returning to her brother's side, she kisses his cheek. "Have a nice time on your not-exactly-a-date. If she's any kind of woman she'll see how wonderful you are and fall madly in love with you instantly. Just be yourself. You know, only more festive." She licks her finger and wipes the smear of lipstick from his face. "If you're free later come by and help us deck the halls, OK?"

*　　*　　*

I will love you until the day I die.

As Dignon walks toward downtown, he remembers Lisa's vow, made to him so many years ago, not long after they'd run off to New York together. They'd only been in their studio apartment for a day or two, and spent the afternoon in bed, tangled in blankets, watching frost form along the windows and listening to the sounds of the city pulsing all around them.

He wonders what she looks like now, who she's become, the forty-two-year-old version. She's probably married and has a bunch of kids — maybe even grand-kids — a house on Long Island and a minivan in the driveway, her dreams of being a famous actress as forgotten and distant as her broken proclamations.

Dignon has often pictured her over the years, rocking a baby in her arms or moving through some spacious, immaculate and meticulously-decorated home, accompanied by a dashing and painfully handsome husband, their life together a Norman Rockwell painting.

I will love you until the day I die.

But I failed you too, didn't I? I wasn't what you needed me to be, what I wanted to be for you, for us. The damage was already done, wasn't it, Lisa? I was already gone, broken beyond repair even then. No amount of hope and love and patience could've fixed me. Not then, not now. You did the only thing you could to survive. You swam away from a drowning man rather than allowing him to pull you under with him.

For some reason, a memory of the super who rented them the apartment comes to him. A slovenly man in his mid-fifties who always had a cigar stub jammed in the corner of his mouth, he told horribly offensive jokes at every opportunity until one day Lisa asked him not to use racial slurs in her presence. He'd laughed uncontrollably, like her request was the most ridiculous thing he'd ever heard. That man would be in his seventies now. He might even be dead. Odd, the passage of time, Dignon thinks. Did that man think about such things? Did he ever wonder where he might be in twenty years? Did he imagine himself an old man or that his life might even be over by then?

Twenty years from now Dignon will be sixty-two. The concept of enduring the same amount of time it's been since he and Lisa were together seems virtually unfathomable to him. He won't make it. Not like this.

The book reminds him it's there, in his hand. He glances down at it without slowing his stride.

I will love you until the day I die.

Blood In Electric Blue

This time, when the words echo in his mind, it is no longer Lisa speaking. It's Bree Harper's voice instead.

And then suddenly, there she is.

As he crosses the street toward the sign advertising *Jerry's*, he sees a woman standing in front of the coffee shop waiting for someone.

Him, she's waiting for him.

It's her.

SIX

He is nearly upon her before she notices him.

In a pleasantly hopeful tone she asks, "Dignon?"

"Ms. Harper?" Dignon holds the book up in evidence.

"Bree, please, call me Bree—hi!" Her dark coat is long and buttoned tight against the cold, a woolen scarf is bundled about her neck, and a black leather purse is slung over her shoulder. She offers a gloved hand, the mist from her breath partially obscuring her face. "Thanks so much for doing this, I really appreciate it. I hope it's not too much of an inconvenience."

He takes her hand. The leather glove is soft but cold. "Not at all." Dignon clears his throat in an attempt to shake off his nerves, and with his free hand, passes her the book.

"Awesome, thanks." Bree glances at the book then resumes eye contact. She is only an inch or two shorter than Dignon, but has boots on, black leather, knee-high ones with fairly substantial heels. There is a disarming air of confidence about her, but not a shred of arrogance. Her salon hairdo, a short, just to the base of her neck

Blood In Electric Blue

razor cut combed straight down in front to the tops of her eyebrows and flared out along the sides of her face, along with her clothes and general sense of fashion suggest she may not be wealthy, but she's certainly not poor like he is either. "You know, I'm still trying to figure out how it ended up at the park. I must've lost it and —"

"Yeah, maybe someone else found it and left it there. It was just sitting on a bench when I found it." A spasmodic smile jerks across his face. Even in the cold, he can smell her perfume. It's very feminine but not overpowering like many fragrances are. Instead, it captivates him like a narcotic. Dignon breathes it — her — in. "Like I said on the phone, I thought you might want it back since you had your name in there and all."

She smiles, revealing beautiful teeth behind equally tantalizing lips covered in a glossy pink lipstick that gives them the look of being perpetually moist. It is difficult to gauge her age, she could easily be anywhere from late twenties to middle thirties. "I probably shouldn't do that, you never know today, right? Luckily you found it and not some deranged serial killer!" She belts out the same contagious laughter he heard on the phone. "Look, can I — I mean I feel like I should — can I buy you a cup of coffee or cocoa or something?" She angles a thumb at the coffee shop behind them. "We're here, we might as well."

"You don't have to do that."

"I know, but I'd like to." Magnificent violet eyes, encircled in black, widen innocently. "OK?"

Dignon stands there smiling like an imbecile. Say something, you ass!

"Come on, it's the least I can do," she insists. "Besides, it's freezing out here."

"OK," he finally hears himself say. "Thanks."

Once inside, they are met by a welcoming blanket of

heat. Bree Harper crosses the room with a confident and deliberate stride, a bounce in her step. Dignon follows, self-consciously looking around enough to notice several glances from other patrons. Few fail to notice her, and some even stare without attempting subtlety. He lowers his eyes and continues on until they find a small table near the front window. A college-age woman appears instantly and takes their order. Bree orders for them, asking for two medium hot chocolates with whipped cream. The shop is packed, and the buzz of conversation nearly drowns out the soft acoustic guitar arrangements playing from flat circular speakers installed in the ceiling. The entire place basks in the aroma of numerous coffees and teas.

As Bree removes her coat and lets it lay over the back of her chair, Dignon realizes he has never sat down in *Jerry's*. He's been here many times over the years, but has always gone straight to the counter, ordered and left.

"It's really hopping tonight, huh?" she says, peeling off her gloves.

"Yeah, it's usually busy in here." A maelstrom of emotions fire through him all at once. She's amazing, as enchanting as he knew she'd be, beautiful, funny, smart, and completely out of his league. A woman like this would never see him as a romantic interest, it wouldn't even occur to her in any serious context, and now he wishes he'd never allowed himself to think she might.

"Have you lived in town long?" she asks.

"Long time, yes."

"Are you from here originally?"

"I was born in Monroe, a little town about half an hour from here. I moved to New York City for a while back in my early twenties, but that didn't last long and I moved back. I settled here and I've lived here ever since." *Easy, take it easy. Don't ramble on and on, it was*

Blood In Electric Blue

a simple question. "What about you?"

"Actually, I just moved here a year ago," she tells him. "I was an Army brat growing up. We lived all over the place. I've had wanderlust ever since."

"That must've been hard."

"Sometimes it was. Just when I'd get used to one place and make friends and know my way around school and whatnot, my father would get stationed somewhere else and off we'd go. In a sense it was a good experience because I'd seen most of the world by the time I was sixteen or so, but in other ways it made for a difficult life, you know? I was never able to put roots down anywhere. And with what I do now I still can't."

Answer her. Say something witty, you stupid bastard. "Roots are overrated."

Bree raises her eyebrows, as if she isn't sure she heard him correctly. Then another spectacular smile spreads across her face. "You may be right on that one, Dignon."

He loves the sound of his name coming from her lips. "So, you still move around a lot then?"

The waitress returns, delivers the hot chocolates and moves away. Bree holds the Styrofoam cup with both hands. "Yeah, it's in my blood, I suppose. I must be part gypsy or something." She laughs.

Dutifully, Dignon laughs too. "What do you do?"

"I'm an administrative coordinator. Adult Ed, GED and English-As-A-Second-Language are my areas of expertise. It's a government gig, I go to various programs throughout the country, help them set up local offices in conjunction with state and federal programs, oversee them until everything is in place and running properly and then it's off to the next town." She raises the cup to her mouth and takes a cautious sip. "Wow, that's hot."

Dignon glances at his. "How long do you think

76

you'll be here?"

"It's hard to say for sure. Depends on how the program comes together." Returning the cup to the table, she sits back, and with her index finger, casually slides a renegade strand of hair from the side of her face. In the bright light of the shop, her brown hair sports considerable ginger highlights. "What do you do?"

He draws a deep breath. "I'm between jobs right now, but I worked for *Tech Metropolis* for years."

"Oh, I love that place. They have so many neat toys."

"Yeah," he smiles gratefully. "I was in the shipping and delivery department over there and—anyway—there was a problem and I'm on a leave right now."

"Leave?"

He fidgets a bit. Stay calm, just breathe and talk to her. "There was an incident with my partner and…he was killed."

"He wasn't the guy who was shot, was he?"

"Yes."

"Oh my God," she says, a hand to her mouth. Her fingers are slender; the nails professionally manicured and painted a shade of pink that matches her lipstick. "You're the guy who worked with him and was there when it happened? That was you?"

"Afraid so."

"I remember when that happened. I read about it in the paper, saw the reports on TV."

Distant memories of the shotgun clicking empty remind him he will never have the luxury of forgetting that sound. He shrugs, unsure of what to do.

"I'm *so* sorry." Bree reaches across the small table and touches his hand. "He was killed right in front you, wasn't he?"

Her touch sends chills through him. The tension is gone. "Yeah, he was."

Blood In Electric Blue

"You poor thing, that must've been awful." Her fingers gently pat the back of his hand. "Is that guy still locked up, I hope?"

"He's in a psychiatric hospital."

She sighs, sits back and takes her hand with her. "That wasn't very tactful on my part, was it? Obviously it's a very traumatic thing for you, I should've—God—sometimes I should just learn to shut up."

"It's OK, you didn't know." He somehow finds the courage to look her dead in the eye. "It's behind me now anyway. I just haven't figured out yet what I want to do from here."

"Well it's probably best that you take your time and put some distance between yourself and all that. Such a tragedy, I'm so sorry I got us into this, I—"

"You don't have to keep apologizing, it's OK, really." Dignon picks up his hot chocolate and drinks some. It burns his mouth but he swallows it anyway. He notices *Mythical Beings in a Mortal World* on the table to Bree's right. "That's a really interesting book."

"Did you read it?"

"Not exactly, but I scanned through it and—"

"Oh God," she says suddenly, her eyes turned to the front window next to them and the street beyond. "I do not need this tonight."

Dignon sees a man standing in the front window glaring at them, his jacket hanging open despite the cold. He is unshaven and looks wildly agitated, his dark hair mussed, like he just rolled out of bed. He appears to be about Dignon's age, perhaps a few years younger.

"Sorry, but I better go." Bree pushes her cup of cocoa away and slinks back into her coat. "It was really nice meeting you and thanks again for returning the book."

"OK," he says meekly. "Are you—is everything all right?"

"Ex-boyfriend," she says, standing. "We broke up and he isn't taking it well."

The man points through the glass at Dignon and says something, but his voice is muffled through the window. "He looks really mad." Brilliant analysis, you idiot, do something. "Is he, I mean, is there going to be a problem or—"

"It'll be fine." Bree smiles again, though nervously this time as she collects her gloves and pulls them on. She gives the man in the window a dirty look then slings her purse over her shoulder and refocuses on Dignon. "I really need to go. I don't want him coming in here and causing a scene. Take care, OK?"

"You too."

She turns and leaves, moving quickly through the throng of tables. Dignon watches as Bree and the man move past the front window. They begin to argue.

Dignon pulls his coat on, tosses a dollar tip on the table and realizes Bree left the book behind. He scoops it up and hurries out after them, but the frigid temperature sobers him immediately. What the hell are you doing? This is none of your business, stay out of it.

The man's voice echoes up the street. Dignon follows them, sticking close to the building until he sees them stopped at the next block. The man flails his arms around dramatically as he screams at her, but Dignon can only make out every third or fourth word. A few people slow their pace and glance at the couple but the man continually flashes them angry smirks and everyone moves on. When Bree turns away from him and waves a hand at him dismissively, the man grabs her by the arm none-too-gently and jerks her around so that she's facing him again.

Dignon walks quickly across the street to the next block. "Excuse me, Ms. Harper?" he calls, holding the book up so she and the man can both clearly see it. "Ms. Harper?"

They turn in unison and look at him.

"Ms. Harper, you forgot your book."

Bree nervously looks back and forth between Dignon and the man.

The man squares his shoulders and positions himself between Bree and Dignon. "You need to get out of here, pal. Just turn around and go the other way, you got it?"

Ignoring him, Dignon leans to the side a bit so he can make eye contact with Bree. "You forgot your book."

"Thank you," she says, but as she tries to push past the man and take it, he blocks her path.

"Stay away from her," the man snaps.

"Kyle, stop it." She looks to Dignon. "Thank you, it's OK, I'm—I'm OK."

"Are you sure?"

"Yes, it's fine, just—"

"Hey!" The man steps closer. "You hear me, dipshit?"

"My name's Dignon," he says, hopeful his fear hasn't manifested in his voice.

"What the hell kind of faggot name is that?"

"Leave him alone, Kyle."

"You shut the fuck up," he snaps, pointing a finger at Bree. "What do you think, she's gonna be your girl-friend? Is that what you think, you poor pathetic lard-ass?"

Bree shakes her head helplessly. "For God's sake, stop it."

"Look, we just met," Dignon says, showing him the book. "I have a book of hers and—"

"Get out of here." The man moves so close their faces nearly touch. "Go."

"It's OK, Dignon," Bree tells him, her face flushed.

Greg F. Gifune

"Just do what he says, it's OK, really. I'm so sorry about all this."

Everything in his being tells him to run, to get the hell out of there and to mind his own business. But he stands his ground.

"Are you deaf?" Kyle snorts at him like a bull. "Get out of here."

"You don't have to threaten me, it's—it's not necessary, OK?"

"If I was threatening you, you'd know it."

Dignon drops his hands to his sides so the man won't see them shaking. "Are you sure you're all right?" he asks Bree. "I can call somebody if—"

"You got no idea who you're fucking with. Get moving while you still can." Kyle stabs a finger against Dignon's collarbone with such force it knocks him off balance. "One day you'll thank me."

Through the pain firing across his shoulder, Dignon sees in this man everyone who has ever made fun of him or bullied and pushed him around. But he hasn't been in a fistfight since elementary school, and he lost that one decisively. This man is physically fit and looks as if he knows how to handle himself in a brawl. Dignon's heart pounds and he feels a bit lightheaded. "I don't want any trouble, but I—"

"Go home, Kyle." Bree steps between them, her back to Dignon. "Please. Please, just go home."

He stares at her for a long while then glares over her shoulder at Dignon. His face contorts in frustration and rage unlike any Dignon has ever before seen. "I fucking warned you," he says, spitting the words at him. "You're gonna be sorry you didn't listen, fat boy."

Kyle turns and storms off. He does not look back, but when he reaches the next block he breaks into a full run, his coat flapping behind him in the winter wind.

81

Blood In Electric Blue

"Are you all right?" Dignon asks. He feels ridiculous, she had to save him.

"I'm absolutely mortified, but I'll live." Bree frowns. "He must've followed me here. Kyle has some rather serious anger issues."

"You think?"

She laughs, and Dignon feels useful again. "I can't believe he did that."

He looks down the street. "Do you think he'll come back?"

"I doubt it."

"Maybe I should—do you want me to walk you home?"

"Oh, that's sweet, thanks, but it's not necessary."

"I really don't mind."

"I'll be OK."

Before he can say anything else, Bree leans in and kisses him on the cheek. It is such a quick gesture he nearly misses it. The lingering feeling of her lips on his face is all he has to hang on to.

"Take care," she says, "hope we see each other again some time."

Dignon nods, speechless.

It isn't until she's crossed the street and is out of sight that he realizes *Mythical Beings in a Mortal World* is still clutched in his hand.

SEVEN

Before Dignon reaches his apartment, he notices Nikki sitting on her steps next door, absently smoking a cigarette while watching his approach. Her duster is draped over her shoulders like it's been tossed there from above, and her spiked hair juts out from various angles, thorny colors even more vivid at night. She offers a less than enthusiastic wave. "Hey."

"Hi." As he slowly climbs the steps to his building he realizes she's still wearing the boots. "How's it going?"

She crosses her legs at the knee, pushes her bottom lip out and expels a stream of cigarette smoke into the air. "It's going."

"Are you OK?"

"Peachy."

"Good, you didn't hurt yourself earlier then?"

Nikki rolls her black veiled eyes. "OK, so like, did every fucking living being on the eastern seaboard see me fall on my face today, or what?"

"Sorry, I just—I'm glad you're OK, that's all."

"Thanks," she says begrudgingly. "Here's hoping I pull through."

Blood In Electric Blue

He looks at his hands. Lights from Mrs. Rogo's tree bleed through the front window and stain his flesh with multihued swaths. There is something troubling about this. "OK, well, goodnight then."

"Hey…" Nikki points at him with what's left of the cigarette. "Sorry, what is it again? Dabney?"

"Dignon."

"Right, Dignon. I scraped my hand and wrist pretty bad, but I'm OK. It was nice of you to give a shit. I didn't mean to be a bitch, it's just my nature. Don't take it personally." She takes a final pull on the cigarette then flicks it out onto the sidewalk. "Looks like you've got a little boo-boo there yourself."

He glances at the Band-Aid on his finger. "Yeah, I…"

"It's been one of those weeks. Freakin' Christmas season, that's what it is. It makes me so bat-shit it's not even funny. Well, it *is* funny, but in more of an I-want-to-stab-myself-in-the-eyes-with-scissors kind of way, you know? I keep hoping for something to save me so I don't have to go to Pennsylvania to see the folks. Something fun, you know, like a nuclear winter or the return of the black plague." She pulls the duster in tighter around her. "Isn't it supposed to snow tonight?"

"Yes," he answers, realizing this is already the longest conversation they've ever had with each other. "But they said on the news it won't start until after midnight."

"Maybe we'll get a blizzard, a horribly crippling blizzard."

"It's only supposed to be a few inches, actually."

"Shit." She casually points at the skyline. "That factory's probably slowly poisoning us all to death anyway. If only they could step it up."

Dignon looks over his shoulder at the smokestacks in the distance and the clouds spewing from them. "It never stops," he says, almost to himself. "It's always going. For years the smoke's just been steadily pouring out of there."

"Hey, better living through chemicals," Nikki scoffs. "Supposedly that's why the shit comes out of the stacks white, all the toxic stuff's cleaned up first, before it comes out and hits the air."

He's always considered the clouds more a gray color than white, but nods regardless.

"That's what they say anyway. I don't believe a word of it, though, do you?"

"I don't know."

"Think about it. Nobody's even really sure what the hell they do in there or what goes on in that place. I know it's some sort of government sponsored plant, but ever notice how all the employees are out-of-towners and nobody ever questions anything? It's like we're all under some kind of freaky mind control or something so we don't make waves. And don't even get me started on the whole aesthetic angle. Who builds such an ugly-ass factory right along the shoreline like that? What are we in a Kafka novel? Hardly. Maybe the smoke's slowly turning us all into cockroaches, though, that'd be cool." She scratches her chin with short fingernails painted black. "I bet that's really what's in the smoke, some drug we're all breathing in that keeps us in line. And we don't even know it."

"I'm pretty sure it's just a chemical processing plant."

"Why are they so secretive then?" Her eyes widen. "Maybe it's a cover for something like the Stasi back in East Germany before the wall came down. The *Ministerium für Staatssicherheit* was a secret police force, and it had thousands of private citizens working for them and spying on their neighbors and shit. Nobody trusted anyone and everybody was afraid all the time. Sound familiar?"

Blood In Electric Blue

"Yeah, kind of, I guess. Right now I have to go though."

The jingle of Dignon's keys draws her attention away from the smokestacks. A silver piercing in her eyebrow catches the moonlight and reflects it back at him. "It's cold, I should get inside too," she sighs. "Nice talking to you Digby."

* * *

Dignon is so hungry he feels weak. The entire building smells like pork chops. Another of Mrs. Rogo's meals has apparently gone unattended. Her Christmas music is again in full swing. It's Rosemary Clooney this time.

Mr. Tibbs hops up on the kitchen table and watches Dignon as he stands in the light of the open refrigerator, staring at the nearly empty shelves. He closes the door then checks the freezer. A small frozen pizza falls out. He catches the box, closes the freezer and shuffles over to the microwave. As the pizza cooks, he pets Mr. Tibbs, who walks back and forth along the edge of the table, raising his haunches to meet Dignon's hand as it slides from his neck down along his back to his hindquarters. But for the lamp near the easy chair in the other room, the apartment remains dark. Dignon wants it that way and feels more comfortable in low light for some reason. "Quite a night," he tells the cat. Mr. Tibbs sits and awaits further information. "Bree's amazing. She's beautiful, smart and really sweet. But not in that icky way, it's genuine. You'd like her, dude." He scratches his head, wonders if he'll ever see Bree again. After all, he still has her book, he could use it as an excuse to contact her again, maybe make a joke about the whole thing. But he's sure she would never consider him anything more than a friend. "She could have any man she wants, why the hell would she want me?"

The microwave answers with an annoying beeping sound. The pizza is done.

"Thing is, Tibbs, I can't stop thinking about her."

Dignon opens the oven, pulls the pizza out and slides it onto the counter. It smells better than it looks. His stomach growls and grumbles with anticipation, but those sounds stop him cold. Earlier he changed into nightclothes, a pair of sweatpants and a sweatshirt. Even in loose clothing, his gut is evident, hanging there like a gargantuan tumor. He slowly raises his shirt, looks down at it. Stretch marks slash across his skin like knife wounds, scarring him. With his other hand he reaches beneath the flesh, lifts it up then releases it, watching as it bounces back into position and jiggles like gelatin. Carefully pulling his sweatpants out and away from his body, he realizes that unless he has an erection he cannot see his penis. He releases the pants then cranes his neck so he can look back over his shoulder at his rear end. It's misshapen and sloppy. He wasn't heavy as a child or as a young adult, so when did this dramatic transformation in his body take place? Surely it didn't happen overnight. It crept up on him, a gradual process that began inside him, in places he couldn't see or hear or feel, and by the time he realized what was happening, it had already overtaken him and turned him into something other than what he'd been before. Like death, he thinks.

He remembers every insult Bree's ex-boyfriend used on him. He hadn't called him ugly or short or stupid or even bald. He called him fat. As if this somehow defined who he was, not just how he looked. Lard-ass...fat boy...

Dignon tosses the pizza on the kitchen table. "It's pepperoni," he tells Mr. Tibbs. "Knock yourself out."

As the cat closes in on the food, Dignon grabs a beer

Blood In Electric Blue

instead then picks up *Mythical Beings in a Mortal World* and flips through it while making his way to his chair. He sits down, sips his beer and continues to scan the various entries in the book.

This is the one that begs to be read:

~SIRENS~
Thought to have first appeared in The Odyssey, these crea-tures, sometimes referred to as nymphs, other times as fiends, are famous for their unearthly beauty and for the lure of their song. Sirens' singing is so enticing it often lures sailors to rocky shorelines where they shipwreck and drown. To avoid this, Ulysses once had his crew plug their ears with beeswax. Temptresses who possess great knowledge regarding the secrets and mysteries of life, Sirens use beauty rather than violence to destroy those helplessly drawn to them. Around 1400, a Siren was allegedly briefly captured in Europe. Astonishingly attractive, she appeared to be human, but was not, as she could live in water as well as on land. Sirens are immortal, except for those rare occasions when a man fails to fall under their spell. When this happens, a Siren will throw herself into the sea as a means of escape, but will instantly be transformed to stone.

He remembers vague nightmares...flashes of fog-covered ocean...

A sudden urge to urinate forces Dignon up and out of the chair. As he passes the kitchen table, Mr. Tibbs looks up from the remains of the pizza and meows gratefully, grease and cheese staining his whiskers.

Without bothering to turn the bathroom light on, Dignon stands over the toilet and pees, listening to it splash the water and echo across the tile walls and floor. A brief bout of dizziness comes and goes. On an empty stomach, the beer is going straight to his head. With a sigh, he turns and looks out the window to his left.

Greg F. Gifune

Directly across the small space between the buildings is Nikki's apartment. Only one window faces his bathroom, and in all the time they've lived next door to each other, with the exception of particularly hot and humid summer nights, he can never remember the shade being anything but drawn.

Until tonight.

Though the light is on in her apartment he can't make out much beyond a dingy bureau and a closet without a door. A shadow moves along the wall as he finishes peeing. He shakes himself off then pulls his sweats back into place and stands in the dark, watching the shadow move slowly closer to the window.

Nikki steps into view with a pile of laundry in her arms and dumps it on top of the bureau. Her head bobs rhythmically, indicating she's listening to music.

Dignon doesn't flush the toilet. He doesn't move. He barely breathes, worried — however illogically — that she might somehow hear him through the buildings and open space, through the night.

Watching his neighbor perform the mundane task of putting various items of laundry away in bureau drawers transports him back to New York City, all those years ago.

There was a large apartment building directly across from the second floor studio he and Lisa were renting, and soon after they moved in he began noticing a woman in one of the apartments. She was a professional of some sort. Always nicely dressed, she worked banker's hours, normally leaving about eight-thirty in the morning and returning home about five-thirty. Dignon was sure he had neither a lascivious design on the woman, nor any particular interest in her at all, as he was madly in love with Lisa at the time. But there was something fascinating about watching this young woman come and go, and

89

Blood In Electric Blue

contemplating who she was and what her life entailed. A few times he had watched her return from work, quickly undress then throw casual clothes on and head back out. He often wondered why she was always alone. She was quite attractive, yet he never saw her with anyone, as if she kept her apartment as a separate and private place apart from the rest of the world. Sometimes he tries to imagine what became of her. They'd had this odd relationship of sorts without her even realizing it. She never knew he existed, and yet, he still sometimes thinks of her to this day. She'd be in her forties now. Does she still live in that apartment building? Does she still live alone? Does she still live at all?

As he watches Nikki putting clothes away he wonders how much of life happens outside one's awareness. For all he knows, someone could be watching him at that very moment too, wondering the exact same thing.

Another memory finds him. One morning a few years ago, Wilma had invited him to breakfast. He'd been running late doing some errands and stopped at a payphone to call her and let her know he'd be there soon. As he stood listening to the ringing on the line, a man walking past on the street made eye contact with him. Dignon had never seen the man before, and never saw him again, but had maintained eye contact with him until he'd disappeared into a crowd of people near the end of the block. There was something about him, something in his eyes, sorrow perhaps, that he's never forgotten. To this day he has no idea why he felt compelled to return this man's stare, but it seemed the right thing to do at that moment in time. It seemed necessary. For them both. This strange brief connection, there then lost. Was it significant? Was it simple chance, completely meaningless? Or was it a sign, just one more piece of an intricate puzzle

90

spanning his entire life, carefully planned out ahead of time by greater, more powerful forces and designed to be fitted together gradually over time, never making total sense until the puzzle is completed?

Even tonight was curious. Why had he and Nikki had their lengthiest conversation with each other ever on *this* night specifically? And why was the shade to that room lifted in winter for the first time in the three or four years she'd lived there? Could these things all be coincidences, or were they more signs?

"Signs," he whispers. "Signs of what?"

Nikki reaches deep into the pile of laundry and pulls out what appears to be some sort of undergarment, a slip, or something similar. As she pulls it free of the pile, Dignon notices a peculiar discoloration to the otherwise silky white fabric. She holds the garment up to the light, inspecting it nonchalantly, as if for lint. The lower half is soaked with what appears to be blood.

His stomach feels like someone has reached inside him and squeezed his intestines, and his heart hammers his chest.

Nikki grins, brings the bloody garment to her face and rubs it across her cheeks, nose and chin, covering herself in a shiny crimson mask.

With a hand to his mouth, Dignon slams shut his eyes.

After a moment, he forces them open.

His neighbor is still there, still putting away her laundry. She holds a red shirt up to her face and smells it, perhaps enjoying the fragrance of a particular detergent she uses. There is no blood on her face, no blood-stained undergarment, no blood at all.

Dignon trembles in the darkness a moment, shaken. He runs his hand from his mouth up over his forehead and exhales a deep breath. "What the fuck," he whispers.

Blood In Electric Blue

His vision refocuses as an image emerges from the dark windowpane to reveal an anemic ghoul. It takes several seconds before he realizes it is his own reflection in the glass.

Something blinks and the reflection is gone.

The light in Nikki's window has gone out.

*   *   *

It is very late at night, but still no snow. Dignon walks the street bundled in a heavy winter coat, a knit hat pulled down over his ears to help ward off the icy winds blowing in off the ocean. But for the factory, the city is quiet, asleep. He has no precise recollection of leaving his apartment and coming here, but Dignon finds himself standing near the tall chain link fence that surrounds the factory, staring blithely at the smokestacks. Along the top of the fence is barbed wire, and a bevy of surveillance cameras are mounted on the buildings within the cordoned off complex. A small security hut just beyond the locked front gate sits empty and dark. From his position on the sidewalk, Dignon can see lights on through a few of the tiny windows near the roof of the factory, but little else. Could Nikki be right? Could there be something horrible happening inside these gates, some unspeakable conspiracy?

As if in response, a door to a small trailer next to the main building opens and a man dressed in security garb saunters out, struggling to get his utility belt secured around his waist as he makes his way across the lot to the fence. He is an older man, perhaps in his sixties, his hair thinning and gray. "Can I help you?" he asks while still quite a distance away.

Once the guard reaches the other side of the fence, Dignon answers him. "I'm just out for a walk. I was watching the smokestacks."

"At two-thirty in the morning? Move along. We got laws against loitering."

"But I'm on a public street."

The guard smiles condescendingly. "Is that a fact? A public street, you say?" With his belt now properly fastened, he reaches for a long nightstick dangling from one of the loops and pulls it free. An enormous ring of keys suddenly appear in his other hand and he moves toward the lock on the front gate. "Let's just see about that."

Dignon takes a step back, toward the road. "What are you doing?"

Lights suddenly appear behind him, bathing the security guard in blue.

A police cruiser has pulled up along the curb behind Dignon. A young officer with a buzz cut gets out, says something quickly into the radio transmitter on his shoulder then waves to the guard. "Evening, Johnny."

The guard puts the stick and keys away. "Evening, Roy."

"We got a problem here?"

"No," Dignon answers for him. "There's no problem. I was just—"

"I observed this young man staring at the facility in a suspicious manner, so I came out to see what he wanted. Told me he was out for a walk. I asked him to kindly move along, and he told me he was standing on a public street."

The cop glances at Dignon with a disgusted expression. "OK, Johnny, I'll take it from here."

"Thanks, Roy." The guard heads back to the trailer from which he came. "You have a good evening now."

"Will do, you too." The cop gives a bored sigh. "Gonna need to see some ID there, bud."

Blood In Electric Blue

"I don't have it with me. I was just out for a walk."

"Come here."

"Excuse me?"

"Come *here*." He points to the section of pavement in front of him as if summoning a disobedient dog. When Dignon complies, the cop reaches for his handcuffs. "Turn around, put your hands behind your back." As Dignon does as instructed, the policeman explains, "You are not under arrest at this time. This is strictly for your safety and mine." He slaps the cuffs across Dignon's wrists, clicks them tight then spins him back around so they're facing each other. "Now, let's try again. Do we have a problem here?"

"No, I was just out for a walk, I didn't do anything wrong. I was standing on a public street minding my own business, I have the right to do that, I—"

"Oh, I'm sorry, counselor. I didn't know I was talking to F. Lee Bailey."

Confused and frustrated, Dignon stares at him helplessly.

The cop rolls his eyes and begins patting him down. "Got anything in your pockets I need to know about? Sharp objects, needles, weapons, anything that might stick me or in any manner cause me bodily injury?"

"No."

"Hope not, 'cause if I get stuck it's gonna be the worst night of your life, you read me?" He finishes the pat down. "What's your name?"

"Dignon Malloy."

"Do you live here in town?"

"Yes."

"Yes what?"

"Yes *sir*."

Satisfied, the cop relaxes his stance. "Mr. Malloy, let me explain something to you. It's the middle of the night, and you're out here staring at a chemical process-ing facility. The folks in there work with some very volatile substances. One of the eggheads in there mixes test tube A with test tube B by mistake and *ka-boom*, there goes the neighborhood. That means a place like this could be of potential interest to terrorists and other mal-contents."

"I'm not a terrorist, I—"

He silences him by holding up an index finger and pointing at himself. "Still talking here, which means you don't talk too. You close your mouth and listen instead, you read me?" Dignon nods. "Sorry, I didn't catch that."

"Yes sir," Dignon says quietly, "I read you."

"Outstanding. Now, in these uncertain times we don't take kindly to suspicious individuals hanging around outside places like this. Sends up all sorts of red flags, makes everybody real nervous, jumpy, irritable. See, because the thing is, decent folks who aren't doing anything wrong, they're all either in bed right now, or they're working a nightshift. Know what they're *not* doing? Standing here talking to me."

"I didn't mean to cause any trouble, officer. I'll go straight home, OK?"

"Not tonight you won't." He takes Dignon's elbow and turns him toward the police car. "We're gonna go for a little ride, me and you."

Dignon looks around frantically. No one else is on the street, no one sees him getting into the cruiser. "But I thought you said I wasn't under arrest."

"You're not." The cop places him in the backseat. "Watch your head." He slams the door shut, slides into the front seat and again quickly says something into the transmitter on his shoulder. After a moment, he pulls away, driving unnecessarily fast through the dark, empty streets.

Blood In Electric Blue

Dignon struggles forward, closer to the metal grate separating them. "Sir?"

"Just be quiet, we'll be there soon."

"This is all a misunderstanding, I was only—"

"You know, I could've sworn I just told you to be quiet."

"Where the hell are you taking me?"

"Keep talking and I'll pull over and taser your ass six-ways-to-Sunday."

The streets become darker still as the cruiser turns into a residential area.

Dignon looks out the window, tries to get his bearings. He knows every corridor of this city. Bad, it's a bad area of town with rundown tenements and several vacant and condemned buildings. And then it dawns on him. He knows where they are.

The cruiser pulls up in front of an old tenement. Dignon has been here before. He and Jackie Shine delivered here once. There were children here, and the two older men who had ordered video equipment. He'd reported the people here. The police never did anything about it.

Other than a lone window on the first floor filled with yellow light, the building is empty and appears abandoned.

"Bet you know where you are now," the cop says.

"What's going on?"

The cop gets out, closes his door then opens Dignon's and yanks him out. "Come on," he says, pushing him toward the building. "Let's go, move it."

Reluctantly, Dignon climbs the steps to the front door, the policeman behind him and holding him by his cuffed hands. "What's happening? I don't want any trouble, please don't do this, I—"

"Shut up, you fucking pussy." The cop opens the

door and they step into a dark foyer. A small amount of light seeps from beneath a door to their left, and Dignon can hear muffled voices beyond it. A few feet away, something small moves quickly then shuffles off, but the darkness is too thick for him to make out what it is.

The apartment door opens. Additional light tumbles into the foyer. An older man greets them. Well into his sixties, he exudes an air of superiority and is well groomed, dressed in an expensive suit and tie beneath an open smoking jacket. "Well, look what we have here," he says with an accent somewhere between British and Old Boston. "Isn't this a nice surprise?"

Dignon recognizes the man immediately. He's the same one who answered the door when he and Jackie Shine delivered the video equipment here. He's the same man who tipped them and hurried them out once they'd seen the children.

"I figured you'd remember this one," the cop says proudly.

"But of course." The man beams, flashing unnaturally large white dentures masquerading as teeth. "How could I ever forget the little weasel that dropped a dime on us?"

"Look, I—I don't know who you guys are," Dignon stammers, "but you have me confused with somebody else, I—"

"Caught him snooping into more shit that's none of his business down at the processing planet, you believe this tool? He's all yours." The cop removes the handcuffs, slaps Dignon forcefully on the back then walks back out into the night without another word.

Dignon rubs his wrists and contemplates running for the front door, but he cannot be sure the policeman isn't standing out there waiting for him. He turns back to the man in the suit. "This is all a mistake."

Blood In Electric Blue

"There are no mistakes. Come in, Dignon, join us."

Fear rises. "How do you know my name?"

He leans closer. "I listen, very carefully."

"But no one said my name."

"I'm always listening, Dignon." Despite looking like a dapper elder statesmen in a Graham Greene novel, with his silver hair neatly styled and combed back, his pencil-thin mustache and silk smoking jacket, there is something sick and diseased about this man, something perverse and unholy. "Always." Behind the man, in the apartment, a handful of people in dark clothing mill about, drinks in their hands, their voices hushed. "We all are."

Lightheaded, Dignon leans against the doorframe. "I just want to go home."

A young girl steps from the darkness, startling him. Has he seen her before? Was she one of the children he and Jackie Shine had seen here that night so long ago? She leans against the man's thigh and rests her head against his waist. She is no more than eight or nine and wearing a pair of shorts and a tank top T-shirt completely inappropriate for the time of year. Her hair is dark and cut short, her face and bare feet dirty, and her eyes glassy, vacant.

"We listen, and we wait. That's what we do here."

"*Here?*"

"Tell me, Dignon," the man says, slinking an arm around the child's shoulders and down onto her chest, "where do you think people like me go when they die?"

It is then that Dignon notices the little girl's arms. Her hands have been crudely removed, hacked off with some hideous instrument of torture and death, reduced now to bloody stumps, nubs of bone protruding where fingers should be.

"We're listening while you sleep, while you dream.

Greg F. Gifune

We're in your room right now. Can't you feel us listening from the shadows?"

*   *   *

Dignon awakens, not with a scream or by bolting upright, but slowly, quietly, uneventfully. The veil of sleep recedes like a wisp of smoke and tails off gradually, leaving him flat on his back in bed, tucked beneath sheet and blankets, his head resting on familiar pillows. He feels more uncomfortable, unsettled than afraid, but as always, the fear is there too. The bedroom is dark, there is little moonlight. Mr. Tibbs is snuggled up against him but is also awake. The cat's eyes glisten and reflect the sparse light from beyond the windows. He stares at them intently, as if something unusual lies beyond them, perhaps on the street.

The apartment creaks as Dignon hears what sounds like a low growl. But he is still half-asleep and groggily realizes it is the winter wind blowing through town he's hearing, nothing more. He imagines himself and Mr. Tibbs in a tent in the arctic, rather than the supposed safety of his bed, a furious storm raging all around them, and for a moment this fantasy entertains and occupies his hazy mind. But then he realizes Mr. Tibbs is not staring at the windows.

He's staring at the shadows beneath them.

"What is it, Tibbs?" he asks, his voice a slurred mumble.

The cat turns to him. His eyes blink slowly, as if to say, "I don't know."

Dignon struggles into a sitting position. Pain shoots from the base of his neck up into the back of his head and out across his temples. He feels sick to his stomach and vaguely remembers finishing numerous beers before he staggered off to bed. He coughs, and his mouth instantly fills with an acidic taste, which only leads to further coughing.

Once the fit passes, he throws the blankets off and swings his legs around onto the floor. It's chilly in here. He waits a moment, listens for the furnace down in the cellar. It's on, he can hear it rumbling. Apparently no longer spooked, Mr. Tibbs opts to remain in bed and pushes himself farther beneath the covers.

The nightmare disturbed him, but Dignon is. too drunk, hung-over, or whatever this state he's in is called, to be as frightened as is warranted. Just the same, he knows sleep is out of the question for a while.

On wobbly legs, Dignon walks to the window. Fat snowflakes fall from the sky. The street and buildings — everything — is covered in a fresh sheet of snow. Despite its beauty, he cannot shake the image of the hideously mutilated little girl. She has followed him from there to here, and though he doesn't want to fear her, he does. Why were her hands missing? Why her hands specifically?

A vision of her reaching for him strobes across his mind then vanishes. In the vision, her hands are intact, giving him something to grab hold of while pulling her free from the hell in which she is trapped. But he offers no rescue.

"I'm sorry," Dignon says softly. "I tried, I…"

Help me, Dig. Help me.

But the little girl is gone. It's Willie begging him, needing to be saved, and then his father's hateful voice is back, escaped from the darkness he has tried his entire adult life to banish it to. *It's your fault. You did this to me. You did this to him. You did this to all of us.*

Head pounding, he escapes into the kitchen. With only the small stove light to guide him, he finds the ravaged remnants of the frozen pizza Mr. Tibbs had for dinner still scattered across the table. He drops it into the trash receptacle, noticing a mountain of empty beer bottles in the nearby sink.

He should eat something, but his stomach is too upset and he's slightly nauseous. Wearily, he shuffles over to his chair in the other room and leans against it.

The night is deathly quiet, but for the steadily droning wind, which cries in a manner he has never before heard. Strange, he thinks, it sounded like a growl when he first awakened from his nightmare but is now eerily melodic.

He needs a distraction, something to relax him. Normally he'd read, but he's too bleary-eyed and his headache has gotten no better. He rarely watches television but resignedly finds the remote, collapses into his chair and turns on the modest set. There must be something on even at this hour.

He's never been able to afford cable, but when he worked at *Tech Metropolis* he used his employee discount to purchase a discontinued Panasonic nineteen-inch television and a decent set of rabbit ears. Still, he only gets a few channels, and none with superior reception. There's a commercial on featuring some obnoxiously loud bearded guy prancing around some sort of food processor type thing. Dignon clicks. A dramatic series featuring actors who look to be in their early thirties playing rich Californian high school students appears. Apparently they're all obsessing about an upcoming school dance and someone named Mandy. Click. A Spanish channel pops up next, showing a Mexican soap opera full of large breasted, heavily made-up women and dashing dark-haired men with perfect hair.

He turns the TV off and sits in the dark instead.

The refrigerator hums. The wind croons. Downstairs

in Mrs. Rogo's apartment, he hears a door close. She must be going to or from the bathroom, he assumes. After a moment her toilet flushes. Odd, does she close the bathroom door even though she's alone in the apartment with her dog Schnitzel? He pictures the wiener dog staring at her as she sits on the toilet, and for some reason finds this humorous. He laughs quietly, but it is nervous laughter, whistling past a graveyard.

It is only when he thinks of Bree Harper, when he remembers her face, that he begins to feel a reassuring calmness wash over him. He imagines her asleep in her apartment across town. Or maybe she's awake too. The memory of her sweeps away the nightmare, his childhood horrors, and even the strange hallucinations of Nikki and her bloody laundry.

The rest is gone.

There is only Bree, sweet, beautiful, magnificent Bree, the ethereal song of a winter wind, and the wondrous snowflakes cascading through darkness on the other side of the window.

EIGHT

The madness of his earlier nightmares replaced with dreams more pleasurable, Dignon spends the remainder of the wee hours wrapped in mysteriously idealistic visions of Bree Harper walking with him across sandy dunes. Snow tumbles from the night sky, the Atlantic slams the shoreline and a winter wind blows harsh and loud. Yet neither takes particular notice of the elements. Bree is speaking, telling him something that seems important, but her lips move in silence, the sound of her voice drowned out by the crashing surf. Her hair flies about like a separate living entity, wild and beautiful and free of restraint. As they climb a particularly steep dune, she rests her head against his shoulder. Dignon puts an arm around her and pulls her close, holding her tight as they struggle through the thick sand together. He doesn't understand any of it — even while dreaming it — but he knows one thing for certain. He's happy, truly, helplessly, shamelessly happy. And so is she.

A strange, barely audible electronic pulsing sound echoes across the ocean.

The apartment slowly emerges from darkness, blends

gradually into focus. The sound follows him from the dream, continues to buzz in his ears. He rubs his eyes, realizes there's a symmetrical cadence to it. The phone, it's the telephone. He struggles out of the chair, his back and legs sore from having spent several hours asleep in that position. Sleepily, he snatches the phone from its cradle on the kitchen wall.

"Dignon?"

He attempts to answer but his throat is dry and raspy. He clears it, coughs a bit then says, "Yes."

"Hey, it's Bree Harper."

He knew who it was the moment he heard her voice but pretends to be pleasantly surprised. "Hi."

"Did I wake you? Is it too early to call, I—"

"No, it's OK. It's fine." He paws at his eyes and does his best to sound alert. "You didn't wake me, I—I'm up. I just didn't sleep too well last night."

"I hate it when that happens," she says sweetly. "I had a night like that a couple weeks ago, you know, where you just stare at the ceiling for hours?"

"Yeah," he says, and leans against the refrigerator. And then something occurs to him. "How did you get my number?"

"You're in the book."

"I didn't think I ever gave you my last name."

"When you first called me and introduced yourself you did. Remember?"

His exhausted mind comes up empty, but he takes her word for it. "I forgot."

"I hope it's OK I called. I mean, I know it's kind of presumptuous but I just wanted to talk to you and I didn't think you'd mind." Her tone changes from effervescent to guarded, perhaps even a bit hurt. "Listen, honestly, if I'm intruding—"

"No, it's OK, really. I didn't mean it like that." A

sudden rush of adrenaline fires through him. "Sorry, I'm kind of out of it this morning."

A long pause follows, but he can hear her breathing.

"I just wanted to apologize again for last night," she finally says. "I had no idea Kyle would do something like that and you didn't deserve to be dragged into that nonsense."

"Don't worry about it, things happen."

"I got home last night and realized after all that I'd forgotten to get my book from you." She laughs.

"Yeah, I know, go figure, huh?" He rubs the back of his neck, tries to weaken some of the tension. "I still have it, if…"

"I was thinking if you're not doing anything later, would you like to have lunch with me?"

Stunned, Dignon stares at the floor.

"Hello?"

Answer her, you damn fool. "You mean today?"

"Sure, if you can make it."

"You don't have to work?"

"It's Saturday."

"Oh. Yeah, right, of course."

"So, would you like to have lunch?"

"OK."

"I hope you don't think I'm being too forward or weird or whatever. I know we don't really know each other, but after the drama last night I wanted to do something nice. Here you are kind enough to go to all the trouble of returning my book and you get stuck in the middle of that mess for your trouble."

"It's really OK," he assures her. "It's not a big deal."

"How about we just start again?"

"Works for me."

"Tell you what, you bring your appetite and the book, and I'll take care of lunch. Fair enough? And no psychotic ex-boyfriends this time, I promise."

"That'd be good."

"Do you have a pen handy?"

"A pen?"

"So you can write down my address. I thought I'd make us something and we could just eat here, if that's OK."

His heart nearly stops. "Yeah, it's...fine."

Her tone again shifts to uncertainty. "We can go out if you'd rather, it's—"

"No, it's all right, I—I have a pen."

"Are you sure?"

"Yeah," he lies. "Go ahead."

Bree recites her address. "What time's good for you? Say twelve-thirty?"

"OK."

"Cool. See you then. Bye-bye."

The line clicks, and she's gone. Hesitantly, Dignon hangs up the phone, wondering if any of this can truly be real, or if it's all just an extension of some heartless dream, ready at any moment to dissolve into fantasy and snatch away the feelings of hope coursing through him. He feels guilty for having lied to her again, but there seemed no alternative. How would she react if she knew he hadn't innocently found her book on a park bench, or if she knew he was already well aware of where she lived, and had even at one point stood just outside her apartment building? Still, he wonders, could she really want him, or is he misreading her? After all, lunch to romantic interest is quite a leap of faith. It's entirely possible, if not likely, she doesn't have any ulterior motives and he's reading more into this than is warranted. Couldn't she just be what she seems to be, a sweet and genuinely nice woman reaching out to him, perhaps wanting to be friends? Then again, having a man to lunch at your home you've met once and don't know from Adam is a strange and rather bold move. *Presumptuous,* isn't that the word she used?

He remembers the dream he was having when the phone rang, and it occurs to him that when he first saw her name in the book he'd immediately envisioned them walking together down by the water. And something else…glimpses of the ocean, fog, something moving through the water…

Mythical Beings in a Mortal World calls to him from the table. He opens it to the same passage he last read: *Sirens.*

Mr. Tibbs rounds the corner from the bedroom, eyes bleary.

"What do you think, Tibbs?" he asks, tossing the book back on the table. "Maybe she's a siren, luring me to destruction." The cat yawns and wanders over to his dish as Dignon takes a box of Cheerios from the cupboard and fixes himself a bowl. "I can only hope, huh?"

He's reminded of an expression Jackie Shine used to have: *A woman like that could ruin a man…if he's lucky.*

But his good humor is short-lived. The earlier nightmares overshadow his thoughts of Bree, and he sees the factory, the cop, the older man, the little girl and the tenement again. The images, fresh and disturbingly vivid, flip through his mind like a slideshow, and then just as quickly, they vanish.

Somewhere in all this there's meaning. Dignon is certain of it. Jokes, dreams, nightmares and hallucinations brought on by lack of sleep and food aside, something real is taking place. He can feel it to the very core of his being. Something is happening here, drawing him closer to an answer, or perhaps a climax of some kind. Could all the strange things of late and the odd memories and nightmares be connected somehow, or is it all just a jumble meant to throw him off some greater, more important trail?

He checks his watch. If he showers and gets himself looking presentable within the next couple hours, he'll still have time to go by that old tenement before his lunch appointment with Bree. The concept of returning there is less than appealing, but he feels he has to, and only knows that if he doesn't, things will get worse.

Dignon sits at the kitchen table, and finally, he eats.

The book, just a few inches away, continues to beckon. Crunching Cheerios, he again scans through it. Barring further mishaps, this will likely be his last chance to do so. Most passages are of little interest and fail to hold his attention beyond a few seconds, until toward the back of the book he notices a subtly bent page. Only the very tip at the corner has been folded, such a tiny portion it easily could've happened mistakenly rather than by design. But he checks it anyway.

~DEATH MAKER~

The earliest mention of this concept as a living being is found in ancient Greece, when creatures described as: "Thanatos Kataskevastis" (which literally translated means "Death Maker" or "Death Constructor"), are said to have existed, although in very small numbers. It is believed they are relatively peaceful, sad, isolated and lonely beings, essentially human but damned by the gods, through no fault of their own, to wander Earth while being involuntarily trailed by death. As a result, those around or close to them experience death or destruction as an inadvertent consequence. The Death Maker (or Death Magnet, as the being has been coined in modern Western slang), carries a curse from its ancestors, usually those of a parent. This is a lifelong affliction that begins at birth and ends only when the Death Maker dies. According to legend, they are often sought after, enslaved or destroyed by a

Greg F. Gifune

*myriad of evil beings or practitioners of black magic, who seek
to draw power by possessing the darkness engulfing a Death
Maker's soul. Though melancholy and nonviolent by nature,
given the right conditions, these beings can also be consciously
dangerous and extremely volatile.*

A chill skips across the back of his shoulders. He
stares at the page a while nonetheless, his mind slithering
its way through a labyrinth of possibilities. Why of all
the pages in this book, of all the entries of various
allegedly mythical beings was *this* one marked? Was he
meant to see this? Could it be more than what it appears
to be? Could it be something extraordinary, a commu-
niqué perhaps, intended specifically for him, another
clue waiting to be found?

It's like I'm some sort of death magnet.

Don't say that.

It's true, isn't it? I have been right from the start.

Mr. Tibbs hops up on the table and begins to wash
himself. Dignon finishes the last spoonful of cereal then
slides the bowl over to the cat, who postpones his bath.
He laps up the remaining milk, purring heartily.

Sounds of movement downstairs are followed by a
new wave of Christmas tunes. Aretha Franklin belts out
Winter Wonderland.

Dignon looks to the window. It's still snowing.

*   *   *

Bundled in a heavy winter coat, scarf and knit hat,
Dignon walks to the retail district, hoping to catch a bus
to the neighborhood where the old tenement is located.
As he hurries toward the stop, a large see-through hut on
the corner, he comes upon a man with a gleam in his eye
distributing something to passersby. It's not an

Blood In Electric Blue

uncommon practice for people to be handing out flyers on the street, but this man, a blond with a 1950's haircut, crystal-blue eyes and a dazzling smile, has such a clean-cut, squeaky-clean look so meticulously groomed he stands out in the crowd. As Dignon gets a bit closer, he realizes the man is peddling buttons.

"They're free, please take one," the man says, thrusting one at Dignon. "God Bless the USA!"

Dignon smiles awkwardly and moves on without taking it.

"Sir?" the man calls. "Sir, they're free, take — sir, hey!"

He stops, looks back at the man.

The smile still in place, the man waves the button as if Dignon hasn't seen it. "It's free, please take one. United we stand, right?"

Dignon reads the button. It's an American Flag across which has been written in bold letters: PROUD TO BE AMERICAN. "I'm all set," he says. "Thanks."

"But they're free," the man says.

He nods, continues on toward the bus stop.

"Hey!" The man stomps after him, cuts in front of him and blocks his path. "Didn't you hear me? They're free."

"I don't really wear buttons."

"Well that's not exactly the point." He thrusts it at him as fat snowflakes fall between them. "It's about showing your patriotism."

Dignon glances around uncomfortably. "Thanks, but I don't want one, OK?"

The man's smile slowly vanishes. "So you're not then, is that it?"

"Not what?"

He aims the button at him for emphasis. "*Not* proud to be an American?"

"I didn't — no, I didn't say that, I — look, I have to

110

Greg F. Gifune

catch a bus."

"Could you tell me why you don't want one? It's free, and it's a positive and powerful message about our patriotism and unity as Americans."

Dignon notices a few people slowing but few have taken notice of their conversation. "You expect me to explain myself to you?"

"I'm just trying to figure out what it is that's offensive to you about this. What American wouldn't want to show their pride? Unless they weren't proud or—you *are* an American, right?"

"I'm Canadian," Dignon says, moving past him.

"No you're not." The man continues to block his way. "You're lying."

"Excuse me." He again tries to get by but the man refuses to move.

"Are you one of those Blame-America-First types? Don't you love and support your own country for crying out loud?"

"I just don't want a button, OK? Move out of my way."

"I bet you make fun of people that fly an American flag outside their home or go to church and have traditional moral values." The gleam in his eyes gone, he wrinkles his nose like he smells something rancid. "Sorry I don't have any 'I Love People Who Hate America' buttons, bet you'd wear that one."

Through the snow, the man suddenly looks less than human, more like a mannequin left there mistakenly, with his perfect hair and immaculate clothing. Dignon sighs and holds out a hand. "Fine, I'll take one, all right?"

"No," the man says huffily, finally moving away. "No, I don't think so."

Shaking his head, Dignon continues on until he

111

Blood In Electric Blue

reaches the bus stop. Due to the snow, most of the others waiting for the bus have gathered inside the clear Plexiglas structure. He steps inside as well, and as he turns, sees the man has ducked into a phone booth. With a grave expression, he dials. Seconds later his lips begin to move. He continually glances over at Dignon and then away while talking into the phone.

"Unbelievable."

Dignon follows the voice to a Hispanic woman standing behind him. Perhaps sixty, she is bundled in winter gear and holds two plastic bags of groceries, one in each hand, down along her sides. "The Ken doll," she says, motioning with her chin to the man on the corner. "Unbelievable."

Noticing they're the only two at the stop not wearing buttons, Dignon gives her a halfhearted smile. "I think he's telling on us."

"Probably calling Malibu Barbie, we're in for it now."

The man hangs up the phone, steps out of the booth and removes a small camera from his coat pocket.

"World's going to hell and he's passing out buttons," the woman says, shuffling closer to him and cocking her head toward the wall of the bus stop. "Look at this thing, for instance. They used to make these out of wood years ago, and there was a nice bench for people to sit down on. But nobody could see what was happening inside and people were getting attacked. So now they make them out of this stuff and they're standing-room-only and see-through so people don't get mugged or raped or worse. At a bus stop, can you believe it? What kind of master-mind criminal mugs somebody waiting for a bus?" She rolls her eyes. "Oh that's right, all the folks with big bucks ride the bus, I forgot."

The man holds up his camera and points it at the bus stop.

Greg F. Gifune

"What the hell's he doing now?"

"I think he's trying to take our picture," Dignon says gravely.

A bus ambles around the corner and pulls to a stop in front of them, blocking their view of the man, and his view of them.

Moments later, from his window seat, Dignon watches the man glaring at the bus as it pulls away, his camera apparently returned to his coat pocket. Before they turn the corner and Dignon loses sight of him, the man's perfunctory smile returns, and against an otherwise picturesque backdrop of whirling snowflakes, he resumes his button giveaway.

The bus slogs its way from street to street and neighborhood to neighborhood until it reaches a stop not far from the tenement. Dignon gets off and moves quickly past a small market, across an empty playground and onto a side street. The neighborhood, soiled and forlorn, is the worst in town, and includes an entire block that is deserted, the buildings condemned. With the delivery he and Jackie Shine made more than a year in the past, it takes Dignon a few moments to get his bearings and remember exactly which building it was.

He stands alone on the sidewalk, his breath escaping his lips and bleeding vines of smoke into the air that form a halo above his head, the polluted thoughts escaping his mind in search of clarity and daylight come to life.

It is quiet on this street, the sounds of nearby neighborhoods softer somehow, muted. Dignon is reminded of the retail district before everything opens and how odd it is to see something that should be vibrant and populated, instead sedate and abandoned. But this is different, more extreme, death rather than sleep. Here, catastrophic events have occurred and this is all that's left behind, the buildings shrines to something once relevant

113

but now lost. There is something unnatural about all this, and yet, the city itself is unnatural, a synthetic intrusion to a world of spirits and nature, overflowing with beings obsessed with building walls and roads and piles of concrete to seal themselves off from whatever may have existed here before them, or perhaps to keep even the prospect that such things might still exist farcical and improbable. Regardless, this is a dead zone, a cannibalized limb, its redemption beyond even the intrinsic beauty of snowfall. There are only nightmares here now, Dignon can feel them, hear them, smell them, even taste them as he inhales, draws them in with the tainted city air, just another carcinogen along for the ride.

The tenement is long abandoned. Even back when he'd made the delivery here, it was clear no one actually lived at the address, but the building was in better shape. It has since deteriorated to an extent barely possible, the windows boarded over and marked with spray paint, the door paneled as well, a tattered orange flyer announcing its condemned status stapled to a pair of planks crisscrossing what was once the entrance. Dignon couldn't get inside and look around even if he wanted to. But it's all right, that's no longer necessary.

The banshees have come out to play. They've found him instead.

The snow continues to accumulate, covering the sidewalks and draping the buildings, concealing it all. Through curtains of flakes, a man appears on the tenement stoop. With a subtle nod of recognition, he moves down the steps and onto the street.

It isn't until the man has come much closer that Dignon realizes who it is. How fitting to come across him here, before this rotting monument to misery. He looks much the same as he did years ago. The same black, intense eyes, the same dark receding hairline streaked

Greg F. Gifune

with gray, the same pasty, pockmarked flesh and the same sinewy build. He even remembers the long coat and the lace-up Florsheim shoes he wore nearly every day, the Timex watch with the fake gold face on a black cowhide band. His hands, the fingers, the nails, the wrists, even the smell of his cheap cologne, it's all the same.

Dignon knows he should be afraid, but he's not.

The man watches him with analytical detachment.

"Are you going to speak to me?" Dignon asks him.

"I don't have a lot of time." His voice has not changed. "Where I am, it's like a prison. They don't let me leave for long."

"Am I supposed to feel sorry for you?"

"Not looking for your pity. Just need you to listen."

"Do I have a choice?"

"Once you hear, you'll have to act on it. You won't be able to keep it buried anymore."

"Why's that?" he asks defiantly.

"Because I'm your father, that's why."

"My father's dead."

"I'm paying for my sins, Dignon, don't think I'm not. I can't get away from the things I've done. The fires burn almost all the time, and the flames destroy, but they also purge…eventually." He looks down the street, distracted by something. "I can't say anything more about that."

The desire to attack the man before him is relentless. Dignon wants to tackle him and punch him again and again until his face is an unrecognizable pulp. He wants to see his blood and snot and spittle stain the snow, to hear him moan in agony and beg for mercy. He has no idea how to execute such a beating, but he can feel the rage and violence building in him, a fury he has only allowed himself to feel in tiny increments before banishing it back into the void from which it comes. "I'm not a little boy anymore, you sonofabitch," he says, heart racing. "I'm a man. Do you see me? I'm a man."

"You have to go back and find the truth about when I died," his father replies. "And then you have to make it right, you understand?"

For the first time Dignon sees not just flesh and bone, but all that lies behind it standing there before him. Along with the rage comes something unforeseen that leaves him ashamed and helpless. He feels love. Perhaps not for his father, but for what he wished his father had been, for what he and Willie so desperately needed him to be. Then, and now.

"Running is easy, son."

"Don't call me that."

"It's finding and facing the truth that's hard. That's where the danger is. And believe me, you're in more danger than you realize."

"What am I supposed to do?"

His pale lips twist into a sardonic grin. "Remember."

"You saw to that a long time ago."

Moving away, his father—or whatever it is—strolls quickly toward the end of the block, turns the corner and disappears back into the storm.

He leaves no footprints in the snow.

NINE

He remembers waiting in the snow for some time, frozen on that deserted street. Despite being shaken to his core, the cold eventually snapped his trance. He inspected the neighborhood once more for specters or signs but found nothing. The world had returned, pale, icy and shrill, its secrets concealed in the misdirection of everyday life.

After another bus ride and a few block walk, Dignon finds himself at the front entrance to 36 Borges Lane. Number 18, Bree told him. He does his best to wash the memories of his father's ghost from his mind, but his is a persistent phantom and that's easier said than done. In his coat pocket, Dignon's hand tightens around a small plastic bottle, a prescription for Valium the doctor gave him along with the anti-depressants. With his heart racing and a slight headache still lingering along the back of his skull, he thinks a Valium might actually be a good idea right about now. He's not sure he can face Bree without one, and fears he'll otherwise stare at the building a while then turn around and go home. In response, the voices in his head grow louder, exploring every conceivable reason why he shouldn't go inside and every scenario of disaster that might happen if he does. He knows if he doesn't find a way to either shut them off or ignore them, he'll weaken and turn around. It's happened countless times in the past in situations far more trivial.

Relax, he tells himself. Breathe.

Without removing it from his coat pocket, Dignon pops open the bottle and shakes free a single pill. After working up a bit of saliva, he casually slides it onto his tongue then swallows, forcing it down.

He looks back at the street, unable to shake the feeling that since he stepped off the bus and walked the remaining blocks to Bree's building, someone has been following him. Maybe Kyle, he thinks. Probably, who else would be following him? None of the passing faces look familiar or seem to take particular notice of him however. Whatever's out there watching, it's well hidden.

The sound of a door opening returns his attention to the building. A man stepping through from inside offers a quick smile and holds the door a moment. "Going in?"

Dignon reaches out, takes the door. "Yes, thank you."

The building is as drab and unimaginative inside as it is out. Everything is an industrial tan color. Across from a bank of mailboxes is an elevator, and to its right a door leads to stairs.

Dignon chooses the stairs.

After climbing several flights, he finds himself in a long and shadowy hallway. The only light comes from a window at the far end of the corridor. He finds #18 and stands before it, watching the pinhole in the upper center of the door, wondering if Bree is on the other side peering out at him. A small red Christmas ribbon is fastened around the doorknob. Beyond the door he can hear a hint of music and the vague sounds of movement.

Dignon knocks.

The sound of movement grows closer and the door swings open.

"Hey!" Bree welcomes him with a dazzling smile. "You find the place OK?"

Dignon returns her smile with one of his own. "Yeah, no problem," he says, stepping inside. He retrieves *Mythical Beings in a Mortal World* from his coat pocket and hands it to her. "Before we forget, here's your book."

"Right, we keep forgetting that part, don't we?" She takes it from him and rolls her eyes playfully. "Can you believe this snow?"

"It's still coming down pretty heavily out there."

"Can I get you something?" she asks, escorting him deeper into the apartment. "I just opened a bottle of Merlot, is that cool?"

"Sure." The apartment is immaculately clean and neat, and a fresh scent fills the air, like everything has been recently scrubbed down with an aromatic cleaner. Although a basic and not terribly inspired living space, Bree has done a lot to make it as appealing as possible. The soft music playing is a new age variety, fluid and ethereal. It emanates from the first room, a den, which is tastefully decorated to include a television, stereo, a couch, and a set of oak chairs with matching coffee table. A large bookcase packed full of books fills nearly an entire wall. A laptop computer, off and closed, sits on the coffee table amidst an array of pretty trinkets and knick-knacks. The art is inexpensive but stylish, mostly reproductions of impressionistic Monet pieces. A modest but real Christmas tree stands in the corner, decorated entirely with silver tinsel and tiny white lights.

Bree leads him through another doorway and into the kitchen, where they're greeted by a small table and chairs, a set designed for two, which she has set with cloth napkins and placemats, affordable replicas of designer tableware and wine goblets. On the back wall, above the sink, two large windows overlook the ocean, offering a beautiful view even through the blur of falling snow. "Isn't it great?" She indicates the windows. "The view's what sold me on the place. There are times it's absolutely breathtaking."

He can feel the Valium slowly taking hold of his system. "The whole place is beautiful."

"Thanks." Bree moves to the counter for the bottle of wine. Dressed more casually than the last time he saw her, she somehow manages to still seem chic in a pair of old Levis, western style boots and a heavy pullover mauve sweater. Her hair is up, secured by a scrunchy the same color, and though her makeup is lighter than it was before, rather than diminish her natural beauty, it enhances it. She pours wine into his goblet then hands it to him. "I wasn't sure what you liked so I went with chicken," she says. "I figured everybody likes chicken, right? Please tell me you like chicken."

"I like chicken." Despite already feeling a bit groggier than he'd wanted to, he sips the wine. Bleary is preferable to panicked.

"It's a kind of Italian chicken salad," she explains, pouring herself some wine before returning the bottle to the counter. "I make a dressing with olive oil and balsamic vinegar then sauté small pieces of boneless chicken in it along with garlic, minced onions and oregano. Then I serve it on a bed of fresh lettuce and top it with grated cheese and more of the dressing. It's easy to make and it's so good."

"Sounds great," he says, and then realizing he's still grinning, lets his smile fade.

"It's already done it's just cooling in the fridge. I

serve it cold. Should only be a few more minutes, OK?"
She motions to the chairs. "Have a seat."

He sees her notice the Band-Aid on his finger, her
stare lingering on it longer than seems necessary.
Thankfully, she doesn't ask him about it. He lowers
himself into one of the kitchen chairs and she remains
leaned against the counter. Out of habit, he looks around
for a dog or cat. "Do you have any pets?"

"No, I wish I did, I love animals, but with all the
moving around I do it's not conducive to having one.
They need a solid base, a home, the same way kids do.
Otherwise it's not fair to them."

Dignon can tell she speaks from experience, and he
remembers her discussing her transient childhood the
last time they'd met. "I have a cat," he tells her. "I've had
him for years. Seems like forever, can't imagine life
without him."

"You guys must be close. What's his name?"

"Mr. Tibbs."

"Sidney Poitier fan, huh?"

"A lot of people miss that."

"I'm a movie buff. I especially like the older
Hollywood films."

"Me too. *In the Heat of the Night* is one of my
favorites."

Bree's eyes widen as she takes a swallow of wine, and
then in her best Poitier voice says: "They call me *Mister*
Tibbs!"

They both laugh. It is genuine and Dignon feels
warmth move through him as his body and mind relax.
His usual self-consciousness is weakening. "Thanks for
inviting me," he says softly. "You know, for lunch and
all."

Bree purses her lips as if to prevent herself from
laughing.

Blood In Electric Blue

"What?" he asks.

"Nothing, you're just sweet, that's all. Haven't you ever been invited to lunch by someone before?"

"Not in a long time."

"Well believe it or not I don't normally invite men I don't know over to my apartment. But I do normally follow my instincts, and from the moment I met you they told me you were a nice guy and someone I had no reason to fear or worry about. I just felt this immediate...I don't know...connection, I guess. You seemed like an old friend instead of someone I'd just met." She gently moves her glass in a small circular motion. The wine swirls about within. "So am I right? Are you as sweet as you seem?"

"Afraid so."

"See? Instincts always pay off. Everything happens for a reason."

"Like fate?"

She nods. "I don't believe in coincidences really. I suppose they do occur from time to time, but more often than not, I think things happen exactly as they're meant to. I was meant to lose my book, you were meant to find it. And because of that, we were meant to meet. It's that simple."

"I hope you're right."

"I know it's easy to write off that kind of belief system as wishful thinking. It certainly makes for a far more interesting world if everything has meaning, right? Otherwise there's no point to any of this, it's all just random. I can't imagine a world with no purpose, a life with no meaning. That'd be an awfully cruel joke, don't you think?"

"There's too much beauty in the world for it to be random."

Bree seems to weigh his response before further

122

Greg F. Gifune

exploring it. "You're a deep guy, Dignon. I bet you see and feel lots of things most people don't even notice."

Warmth spreads across his cheeks. "Sometimes."

"I'm the same way. I can be really sensitive. Some days it's overwhelming, you know?"

He does know. He nods, sips his wine.

They're quiet a while.

Just as he expected an apartment far more transient in nature, Dignon also expected one of his usual inept and anxious conversations to take place once he got there. But neither is the case. In fact, he cannot remember the last time he was this relaxed in a new environment or situation with someone he doesn't know. Still, the ease with which Bree moves and speaks and interacts with him results in mixed feelings. He is pleased yet uncertain. Can or should he trust her? Why is she being so nice to him?

"I didn't mean to get all heavy and serious," Bree says suddenly, pushing away from the counter. "I can be such a bore sometimes."

"Not at all, it's kind of nice to have a real conversation for a change."

She finishes her wine and places the goblet on the table, the expression on her face indicating further thought on the subject. "Yeah, it is, isn't it?" With a quick spin she finds the refrigerator door, pulls it open and removes two bowls of salad from the top shelf. "Come on, let's eat."

They sit across from each other and eat their salads in relative quiet. When they speak, it is small-talk. Music plays softly from the other room, wind whistles beyond the walls and occasional sounds of other people and things in the building filter through.

"Delicious," Dignon tells her.

"Glad you like it." Bree pours them each more wine.

123

Blood In Electric Blue

"So tell me about yourself."

He searches his mind, tries to remember their prior conversation at the coffee shop and what he's already told her. "There's not a lot to tell really."

"Do you have any family?"

"One sister, she lives here in town. You?"

"I'm an only child. I don't see a whole lot of my parents these days. They're retired and live in Miami now." Bree munches lettuce. "It must be nice to have a sister."

"Yes, it is."

"What about your parents?"

"They're dead," he says, immediately wishing he'd phrased it more delicately.

"Oh, I'm sorry."

"Don't be, they've been gone a long time. My father died fifteen years ago and my mother before that."

"That must've been awful for you."

Dignon delays the inevitable by taking another bite of salad. "Not as bad as you might think. I never knew my mother and my father and I weren't close."

"What a shame." She puts her fork down, sits back a bit in her chair. "I've always gotten along reasonably well with my parents. I suppose I'm lucky."

"You are. My father hated me."

"Hate's a strong word."

He musters a polite smile. Something tells him to go on, to let her in, to tell her things he has told no one else, things he rarely even allows himself to think about. He feels uncannily relaxed. "When my mother died my father fell apart. She was everything to him. Her death destroyed him and he never recovered. He hated life, hated God and hated the world and everyone in it. But most of all, he hated me."

"How could he hate his own child?"

Greg F. Gifune

"He blamed me for my mother's death."

"Why in the world would he blame you?"

With his cloth napkin, Dignon carefully wipes salad dressing from the corner of his mouth. "Because I'm the one who killed her."

*   *   *

A while later, the salads finished and their wine glasses refilled, they retire to the den. Dignon sits on the couch. Rather than opting for the chair, Bree sits next to him with complete nonchalance. He feels childlike in her presence, transported back to a more innocent time when a girl sitting close caused nervous perspiration or embarrassed uncertainty. The emotional reaction is the same, but physically he remains calm and at ease.

Bree asks many questions. Dignon does his best to answer them honestly. He explains his mother died from a massive hemorrhage while delivering him, and though Bree is quite sympathetic, she strikes him as oddly fascinated as well. She seems particularly interested in how this event affected his family life from that point forward. Dignon paints an accurately dark but rather broad picture of those years, refraining from fully revealing the extent to which his father had sometimes gone.

"My God," she says. "To grow up like that, with your own father blaming you for what happened while already having to deal with the realities of losing your mother during childbirth in the first place, it's—I mean, I—I can't even imagine what that must've been like for you. Your childhood must've been horribly unhappy."

"It wasn't easy."

"But surely you came to understand your mother's death wasn't your doing?"

"When I got older I understood it better, but it is what

125

it is, as they say."

"Was your father abusive in other ways, Dignon?"

He gazes down into his Merlot. "Look, I — why don't we talk about something else, OK?"

"I didn't mean to upset you." Her hand rests on his. "I know we don't know each other very well yet, but I want you to know it's all right. Personally, I've always found it easier to confide in someone I don't know that well. Maybe it's a condition of the way I live, with all the moving around, who knows? But I've found it's sometimes easier and can lead to a deeper relationship because of the trust factor. I don't want to pry or to make you feel pressured, but I want you to know you can talk to me, you're safe here with me and I'd never dishonor your trust. Not ever. OK?"

"OK." Her touch is warm and soft. Dignon wants to collapse into the cushions, to fall against her and return her touch with his own. Instead, he embraces his newfound calm and lets his inhibitions go. "After Willie graduated high school she moved out, went to work and got her own place. The last two years I lived alone with my father are a blur. By then his drinking had gotten so bad he'd fall a lot, and I used to find him passed out all over the house. Soon as I could, I moved to New York City with my girlfriend at the time, Lisa."

Bree removes her hand and crosses her legs. "That must've been exciting, I love New York."

"It was. I'd never been anywhere, and Manhattan was like going to another planet. But I loved it, and besides, it was where Lisa needed to be. She wanted to be an actress and star on Broadway. That was her dream. In high school she was in the theater club and acted in all the plays. It was all she ever talked about, one day being a famous actress."

"Was she any good?"

"She was talented. Everybody thought she'd make it. She always wanted to live and study in New York, so I went with her."

"What did you want to do with yourself back then?"

Dignon has not allowed himself to think of this for years. When it comes to him, like some dusty trinket found in the back of a dark closet, it takes him a moment to process it. "I wanted to be a teacher."

"I work with a lot of teachers. It's a noble profession."

"I never did very well in school. The only class I liked was English and I loved to read—I still do—so I thought maybe I could be an English teacher. For a while I even thought about being a playwright. I'd write the plays and Lisa could star in them. Stupid, I know."

"Why is it stupid?"

"Just dreams, that's all."

"Sometimes that's all we have."

"Well back in reality the plan was to get jobs, then Lisa would take acting classes and I'd enroll in college. She'd become a professional actress and I'd be a teacher and we'd live happily ever after. Never came anywhere near it, though. My father died a few weeks after I moved. Willie found him. He got drunk and fell down the stairs one night, broke his neck. Coroner said he'd already been dead a week or more when she found him. The mailman got suspicious when his mail started piling up day after day, so Willie went to check on him." He looks beyond Bree, as if seeing those faraway days unfolding before him, projected on the far wall. "I didn't want to come home for his funeral, but I couldn't leave Willie to do everything alone so I came back for a couple days and helped her straighten things out. The house was a rental, there was just his old car and the few possessions he had. Willie handled getting rid of all that and

Blood In Electric Blue

I went back to New York. Few weeks later she sent me a check for half of what she got for everything. My inheritance was about two hundred bucks. Whatever she couldn't sell she donated to Good Will." He notices Bree's violet eyes watching him. They're so beautiful they freeze him a moment. "Lisa and I had jobs by then. She was waitressing and I got hired at a bookstore. She started her acting classes and I was just starting to look into schools when it all went bad."

"What happened?"

"She fell in love with her acting coach and that was that."

"She left you?"

"Took her stuff and moved in with him. We'd been together since our sophomore year in high school and she walked away like it was nothing, like we barely knew each other and all the time we'd spent together hadn't meant a thing. I headed back home a few days later. I never saw or spoke to Lisa again."

"Whatever happened to her?"

"I don't know."

"You never tried to find out?"

"I thought about it a few times over the years but never did." He sips his wine. "I had a lot of problems. I can't really blame her for what she did."

"Sure you can."

He smiles, watches her do the same. "Yeah, I guess I can."

"So you moved back here."

"And I've been here ever since. I had a few different jobs then finally landed the delivery position with *Tech Metropolis*."

"Please don't take offense at this," she says. "There's certainly nothing wrong with being a delivery person, but you don't seem like the usual sort of delivery guy,

Greg F. Gifune

Dignon. To tell you the truth you seem more like an English teacher."

"Most of us aren't what we should be. We're just what we end up."

"It's never too late you know."

"I sort of fell into it," he admits. "I never thought I'd work there forever, I figured it'd be temporary. But before I knew it I'd been working there for years. Only good thing was, it made me quit smoking. Lugging those boxes and being out of breath wasn't cutting it. Of course then I gained about a million pounds because instead of lighting up I ate nonstop for a year. Wasn't long after that I realized I was probably going to be working there the rest of my life. If it hadn't been for what happened to Jackie Shine, I probably would've."

"That had to be terrifying."

"I try not to think about it."

Taking the hint, she revisits the previous topic. "So you never met anyone else after you and Lisa broke up?"

"I dated a few women, but nothing serious. I always thought I'd meet someone eventually. When it didn't happen, after a while I just stopped trying." He sits up straighter in an effort to better hide his gut. "I let myself go. More routines, fell into the same kind of thing in my personal life and eventually I got so used to the way things were it wasn't that big of a deal. At least I've always had Tibbs."

"I'll have to meet him one of these days."

"He'd like that."

"What do you plan to do now?"

"Still trying to figure that out. I don't want my old job back, that's over."

"Have you ever thought about going back to school?"

"Not really."

"Maybe you should."

Blood In Electric Blue

"What about you?"

Apparently amused by the question, Bree leans forward, legs still crossed but torso closer to him, her chin resting in the palm of one hand, the glass of wine held down by her waist with the other. "What about me?"

"Have you always done what you're doing now?"

"I had other jobs right after college, but otherwise, yeah."

"Don't you ever get tired of having to move so much?"

"Sometimes, but it can be really interesting too. I've seen so many different and amazing places, known so many fascinating people. I'm always experiencing new things and learning, growing as a person, and that's important to me." The wind whips and the building trembles, reminds them they are not alone in the universe. "But other times it's like when I was a kid and my father would get transferred from base to base. I move somewhere, get settled in, and the minute I get comfortable, make friends and have a life, it's time to go. It can be difficult, but it's the life I've always had, and as you said, we all get used to things and fall into routines, good and bad."

"Have you ever been married?"

"I've been asked quite a few times."

"I bet."

"I've had some serious relationships—and some not so serious—but I've never met anyone I could actually see myself settling down and being with forever. I wonder sometimes if maybe that's just not in the cards for me. Plus, God knows I've made some bad choices when it comes to men."

"After meeting Kyle I never would've guessed that."

"Hilarious." She smirks lightheartedly. "Believe it or not, when I met him he really was nice. He just got so controlling and obsessive about everything it was ridiculous. I don't need that. I prefer an adult relationship, not one that makes me feel like I'm back in junior high with some jealous, testosterone-gone-crazy teenager."

"So now you're testing the waters with balding unemployed fat guys?"

He expects her to laugh. She doesn't.

"Dignon, I've known a lot of people, some nice and some not so nice. One thing I've learned is that what really matters in this life has absolutely nothing to do with all the things we're told and led to believe." She takes her hand, presses it between her breasts. "It's what's in here that counts. It's who you are deep in your soul. The rest of it's all window-dressing, completely meaningless bullshit that at the end of the day is short-lived and facile at best."

"That's true," is what he says, but in his mind he knows the reality is someone like Bree can never be interested in someone like him as anything other than a friend. "But usually the people who figure that out are alone."

"That's why it's nice to have friends."

"Good ole friends."

She seems perplexed by his sarcasm. "Friends is a good place to start, don't you think?"

He makes himself smile, raises his wine glass. "Sure."

"Maybe it's time you allowed yourself some happiness."

"I've never disallowed it. Just can't ever seem to find it, but please don't feel sorry for me, OK? Anything but that."

For the first time Bree's demeanor turns sullen. "You make an awful lot of assumptions. I know it's probably just a defense mechanism on your part, but I'm not out to hurt you and I'm not making judgments or trying to be pious or unrealistic about how the world works at all. I'm just trying to be your friend."

"Why?"

"Is there some reason I shouldn't be?"

Still unable to believe he's been so open and has sustained a conversation of this depth with her, he allots himself some time to think about her question before answering it. "Women like you don't usually pay attention to me."

"Women like me. I see."

"No, don't—I'm not explaining it right."

"You think I'm on some mission of mercy, is that it?" She shakes her head. "I don't know if I should be insulted or if you're just a master of self-deprecation."

Dignon finishes his wine. Stop talking you shit-for-brains, he thinks, you're blowing it. "I'm sorry," he says a moment later. "I don't—I'm not very good at this sort of thing."

"What sort of thing?"

"All of this." Rather than put his empty wineglass aside, he continues to clutch it as a means of occupying his hands. "I've spent a good part of my life feeling like a total nonentity, you know? And then you come along and you're beautiful and smart and funny and I'm used to women acting as if I don't even exist, so this is all a little overwhelming, that's all. In a good way, though, I don't mean anything by it, I'm just not used to anyone wanting to be my friend, much less someone like you and—I'm an idiot, sorry, I—"

"Stop," she says, taking his goblet from him and placing it, along with hers, on the coffee table. "Relax, OK? I told you, this is fate. We were meant to meet and become friends, I believe that. And all because of that silly book, can you imagine?"

"Maybe we're both mythical beings in a mortal world and don't know it."

"Wouldn't that be fun," she says with a wink. "Want some more wine?"

Dignon looks behind them, to the windows in the kitchen. "I'd love to, but I better check on how it's doing out there. If it's still coming down as heavy as it was I should probably get going soon. I don't want Tibbs to be stranded all alone."

"It's sweet the way you love him so much. Most men are too busy trying to be macho to admit something like that. It's refreshing to meet a guy comfortable being open about that side of himself." She cocks her head toward the windows. "Come on, let's have a look."

Dignon is reminded of when he and Willie were children, and how they'd bound out of bed on snowy winter mornings in the hope that there might be enough to call off school. What he and Bree find is the same steady snowfall as before, only now they can hear plows stalking the nearby streets, grumbling about and moving that which has already accumulated in an attempt to keep up with what is yet to come.

"Pretty nasty out there," Bree says. "It's supposed to tail off soon though."

"I better go."

"Want me to call you a cab?"

"I'll be fine." He offers his hand. "Thanks for lunch. I had a really good time."

She smiles, takes his hand. "Me too, I'm so glad we did this."

Though he doesn't want to let go of her, he does, forcing his hand back to his side. Before he can think of something else to say, she leans in and kisses him on the cheek. He smells her cologne and a trace of what might be hairspray, and feels himself blush like some ludicrous schoolboy. "Maybe we could have dinner some time or," he clears his throat, the awkwardness and uncertainty he'd thought conquered suddenly back with a vengeance, "go see a movie or something."

"Definitely," she says, "call me, I'd love to."

She goes to get his coat, and as he returns to the den he allows himself a quick glance at the closed door just off the room. It can only be her bedroom. Something stirs in him and he looks away. The Valium and wine is wearing off. Insecurity and fear creeps back, coils around him like a snake, tightening slowly but powerfully. Maybe his father's still prowling through the snow, he thinks. Or maybe whoever followed him here is still waiting down on the street after all this time, ready to resume their game.

"Are you OK?" Bree appears next to him, holds up his coat.

He nods, takes it from her and slips into it. "Thanks."

"You looked so intense just then. Did I miss something?"

"Just thinking about the walk home," he says as anxiety rises in him. This latest wave has come so quickly he has no time to prepare or defend against it. He has to leave. It's time for him to go. Now, right now. He needs to get outside in the cold air and let it clear his head.

"I meant to ask you before," Bree says as she walks him to the door, "did you ever get a chance to read *Mythical Beings in a Mortal World*?"

She is at once frightening and beautiful. What has happened to change things so quickly? Surely this is an innocent question, isn't it? His mind sprints, tries to make sense of this sudden surge of panic. "Only a few pages," he answers.

"I think I'm going to have another glass of wine and

curl up with it right now. I've read it before, of course, but it's fascinating — if you're into that sort of thing — and this is as good a day as any to stay in and hunker down with a good book."

"Yes," he says blandly.

"Be careful out there." She opens the door, leans against the frame. "Call me, OK?"

"I will."

She studies him. "You sure you're all right? You look a little peaked."

"Just tired." He steps into the hallway. "See you soon."

"Take care."

Dignon can feel her eyes on him until he slips into the pools of darkness at the far end of the hallway.

In the lobby, he looks through the glass doors before venturing out. The streetlights have come on early. A row of them cover several blocks, glowing through the whiteout, beacons in the cold to lead him home. He wonders if somewhere out there someone else is looking at those streetlights thinking the same thing.

His breath collects against the door.

Outside waits the storm, and all it conceals.

TEN

Through the endless white and cold, through the wind and spray of snow, he sees him standing at the corner. Like he's been waiting all this time, a frozen sentinel covered in snow and sleet, hands at his sides, staring straight ahead, a dark smudge on an otherwise empty canvas, he watches.

Still not certain of the man's identity, Dignon crosses the street and slowly approaches the last stretch of pavement before the steps to his apartment. He hesitates then comes to a complete stop just prior to the curb, realizing now who this is. The man's face is caked with ice and snow, his flesh pale, his eyes bloodshot and savaged with dark circles and bags. Though he still looks dangerous if angered—perhaps even more so than before—he has also acquired a look of exhaustion and despondency. Less a man in search of a fight and more one who has already had the fight beaten out of him; it is evident something more has happened since the last time Dignon saw him.

Something horrible.

"You should've listened to me," Kyle says, his voice

raspy and raw, as if he's spent the last several hours screaming. "You should've listened."

"Why are you following me?"

"I knew you'd end up over there."

The street is quiet, typical city sounds absent in the storm. Somewhere in the distance the rumble of a plow echoes, but otherwise, there is silence.

"Look, we..." Dignon glances around uneasily. "We're just friends."

"You're playing around with somebody way out of your league."

"I'm not playing around with anybody."

"There's going to come a time when you'll wish you'd listened to me."

"I hardly know her, OK?"

"But she knows you."

Dignon gauges the distance between Kyle and the steps. If he walks briskly past him he could probably make it to the door before he caught him. But then what? "What do you want?"

"Stay away from her."

"OK."

Kyle moves for the first time, but he's sluggish now, not strong and strutting like last time. "Are you being a wiseass?"

"No, leave me alone," Dignon says before really thinking it through. "I've got enough problems. I don't need you following me around threatening me."

"I'm not threatening you." He takes a step closer. "I'm trying to help you."

"Well thank you, but I don't need your help."

"You've really got no clue, do you?" Kyle nervously scratches his ear, the tip of his finger lingering as if adjusting something within. "She's not human."

"I have to go."

Blood In Electric Blue

"She gets inside you, in your head, under your skin and — and you can't get her out. She drives you crazy. She's all you'll think about day and night until you can't take it anymore and then..." He staggers away then falls against a light post. Again he picks at his ear, and this time pulls free a small scrap of dark substance. He looks down at it with a blank stare. "Have you heard it yet?"

"Heard what?"

Kyle smiles. "When you do — and trust me, you will — get yourself something to block your ears with. I use this." He holds out the tiny glob of material he pulled from his ear. "Beeswax. It doesn't totally stop it because you can still hear a little, but it makes it better."

Sirens' singing is so enticing it often lures sailors to rocky shorelines where they shipwreck and drown. To avoid this, Ulysses once had his crew plug their ears with beeswax.

Astonished, Dignon asks, "How did you know to do that?"

"Same way you learned about it, how do you think?" He pushes it back into his ear, looks in the direction of the corner and squints through the snow. "I'm so god-damned tired."

"The book — *Mythical Beings in —*"

"That's how she does it, with that book. It's no mistake. It's how she draws you in, like bait. She throws the lure out there and sees what it catches. That's how you met her too, right? And let me guess, you thought it was all your idea, didn't you? You think it's just chance or fate, she'll tell you it is if she hasn't already, but it's not, man, it's not."

Rattled and uncertain, Dignon also feels an ironic sense of relief. He's not the only one who has allowed such wild thoughts into his head. But just because Kyle experiences them too, does it mean Bree is what he claims she is: something horrific and impossible that can only exist in the realm of fantasy and madness?

"Get as far away from her as you can and you might still have a chance," Kyle says. "It's too late for me, I can't stop her. I've tried, I can't. She's inside me too deep." He pushes himself away from the streetlight. "I know. You think I'm nuts. I am. She drives you to it, it's what she does. The impossible is what gives her power. Bree Harper is exactly what you think she is, what you know deep in your heart she is, what your instincts are telling you she is. If you don't believe me, look closer, deeper. You'll find things don't add up. She's a liar, it's all a lie. Think about it, man, just stop and *think* about it. Doesn't it all seem to be happening a little too fast, a little too easily? Isn't it all just falling into place perfectly? Doesn't it seem like the whole thing's a big hand-job, a setup?"

Brow knit, Dignon nods.

"That's because it is."

"What are you going to do?"

"Doesn't make any difference now, it's already over for me."

Tiny specks of ice tickle Dignon's face. "We can't stay out here, we'll freeze." He considers Kyle a moment then motions to his apartment. "You want to come in? You could call a taxi or something."

Though suddenly distracted, Kyle seems genuinely touched by the offer. "You're a decent guy," he says, emotion softening his previously callus expression. "You don't stand a fucking chance."

*   *   *

He's gone, devoured by the storm, forgotten.

To be sure, Dignon watches from the safety of his apartment a while longer, but there's no sign of Kyle out there. He turns from the window, goes to the kitchen and gets himself a beer. From the couch, Mr. Tibbs briefly considers him between yawns.

Sealed off from the world on this late afternoon, the apartment is like a tomb sheltering them from the snowstorm. Even Mrs. Rogo's apartment is silent. No Christmas tunes, no food smells, no blinking tree lights in the front downstairs window. She must be out. But in this, where?

Dignon imagines the apartment is a spacecraft that has crashed on an alien planet. Stranded in this strange world of ice and snow, he and Mr. Tibbs must hunker down inside their crippled ship to wait out the storm. But what if the storm never ends?

It's a silly and childish distraction, but also an effective one.

He drops into his easy chair and allows the fantasy to take shape in his mind. It conjures visions of long-ago Saturday nights in front of the television with Willie and a bowl of popcorn, watching old horror and science fiction movies like *Them!* and *Robinson Crusoe on Mars* on a local UHF channel, and a different, far more annoying kind of snow. He allows himself to wander back through those times, and this occupies him for some while. But soon his finger begins to throb beneath the Band-Aid, and other thoughts invade, force him to look elsewhere.

Dignon sips his beer. "Maybe there's truth in mythology," he says aloud, glancing over at the cat.

Mr. Tibbs seems unconvinced.

Dignon tries to remember what the specific entries in the book said about both creatures, the Death Maker and the Siren. Preposterous as it may be, could they be the link he's been searching for, the bridge that could connect and give meaning to the odd events of late?

It's true, after all, that from the moment he saw Bree

Harper's name and phone number in that book he's been unable to stop thinking about her. He'd become instantly obsessed with her. And it's getting worse. She occupies his mind constantly now.

Maybe it's all chemical, he thinks. The post traumatic stress disorder, the lack of decent sleep, all the pills he's been taking — even those he took then abruptly stopped, like the antidepressants, which the doctor warned against stopping quickly — and the heavy drinking. Certainly his mind is blurred by these factors, so is it all mere judgment and perception, or more correctly, a lack thereof?

Is Bree Harper to blame for all of it?

She's not human.

Her beautiful face comes to him. He scratches at himself nervously.

"I don't believe in coincidences," she'd said.

Do you? asks a voice in his head. *Do you believe in coincidences, Dignon?*

He closes his eyes and sees his father's forlorn face staring back at him through the darkness, an escaped inmate roaming free.

Holding up his beer bottle, he watches the liquid through the dark glass and remembers the little apartment in Manhattan, Lisa sitting nude on the edge of the mussed bed with a fluffy white towel in hand, her hair dangling, limp and still wet from a shower.

"Who called?"

"Willie."

"What's wrong?"

"My father…he died."

"Oh, Dignon, I'm…"

Even she couldn't get the word *sorry* out. Because she wasn't sorry, not really, and neither was anyone else.

He remembers Willie's voice on the phone that day.

Blood In Electric Blue

"He's dead."

Nothing more, and spoken in monotone, recited, reported.

"OK," Dignon answered.

No tears, no words of comfort, sorrow or regret. Nothing. Perhaps later, once it sunk in, relief, but Dignon can't be sure the old man afforded them even that much.

I'm paying for my sins, Dignon, don't think I'm not.

"No you're not," he whispers. "I am."

Wind kicks snow against the windows, brings him back to the other night. It had sounded strange then, almost lyrical in an unsettling way.

Have you heard it yet?

The silence bothers him. It isn't right that Mrs. Rogo's apartment is so quiet, that the entire place doesn't smell of whatever dish she's preparing for dinner. Even the typical city sounds are absent. Maybe he and Tibbs really are alone on a strange and barren planet. A ribbon of tension curls around him. Early warnings of panic squeeze his abdomen, crawl into the base of his throat and strangle him.

Easy, he tells himself, *easy now.*

He swallows more alcohol then moves through the apartment to the bathroom. Without turning on the light he puts the toilet lid down, sits in the shadows and watches Nikki's apartment window. Though the shade is still up, which in itself is strange, the room beyond remains dark. Maybe she's at work already. Could be she hasn't even gotten up yet. She works nights so she probably didn't get in until very late. Still, he tells himself, she's there. He can't see her because she's asleep in her bed, but she's there. She's there. She's there. He continues chanting this mantra in his head, focuses on it rather than the panic.

Perhaps as a defense mechanism, he's rather abruptly

drowsy. Sleep seems as good an escape as any, but here? He leans back against the toilet tank, finishes his beer and sets the bottle in the adjacent sink. A row of plastic prescription bottles sit along the back edge. Anti-depressants, Valium, sleeping tablets, anti-anxiety pills, and another old and expired bottle he now stashes his pot in. Fucking drugstore, he thinks. This realization, that his doctor has given him all these things not because he's irresponsible or incompetent, but because in his professional and learned opinion Dignon *requires* these drugs, makes him even more lethargic. His head feels heavy and unbalanced, like if he doesn't continue to make a concerted effort it will loll to the side and dangle as if his neck has broken.

But then, light.

The sudden intrusion filling Nikki's apartment window restores him to life. Unnoticed, early evening has arrived at some prior point, as all else is engulfed in darkness. Dignon sits up straight so his back no longer leans against the toilet. He rubs his eyes. His mouth is dry and mucky. He runs his tongue across his front teeth. They feel coarse and in need of a good brushing.

Across the small divide, he sees the same old bureau, the same closet with no door. Why had the light come on if Nikki wasn't in the room? It remains empty for some time. Dignon waits, watches, breathes…until she finally crosses into the light.

Her normally spiked hair is calmer but mussed, indicating she has rolled out of bed only moments earlier. He's right then, she must've worked last night and slept through the day. She wears only a tiny pair of bikini panties and a white tank top T-shirt that leaves little to the imagination.

Don't look, he tells himself. It's not right, what's wrong with you?

Blood In Electric Blue

But he does look.

Nikki leans wearily against the bureau, a cigarette dangling from her lips as she opens the top drawer with one hand and rummages around inside it a while. Eventually, her hand returns grasping a pair of socks. She slides the drawer closed and whirls toward the window as if startled by a sudden noise beyond it. With sleepy eyes void of their usual harsh and threatening makeup, Nikki squints and takes a hesitant step closer to the window.

There's no way she can see me, Dignon reasons. The darkness hides me.

She slowly runs her index finger along the window-pane, the tip clearing away a thin veil of condensation. And then without warning she flattens her palm against the glass and begins wiping at it furiously until the window is completely clear. Her breasts strain against the tight T-shirt, her nipples long and stiff.

Dignon blinks rapidly, clearing a montage of images firing through his mind.

Nikki laughs, butts her cigarette in an ashtray on the bureau then leans closer to the window and licks the pane, her tongue pink and moist and flicking back and forth.

Behind her, a dark shape moves into the room but remains far enough in shadow that Dignon cannot make out any particular features.

He stands to relieve the tightness in his pants and also to get a better look, moving slowly so as not to draw attention to himself. And yet, the way Nikki stares across the way, he'd swear she *could* see him. Though he feels ridiculous, he has to be sure, so he raises a hand and offers a slight wave.

Rather than respond, Nikki continues licking, and when she's apparently had her fill, moves back a step and inspects the window with a furtive smile.

Dignon swallows, feels his heart punch against his chest.

The figure behind her moves into the light with a slow, seductive gait. The shadows part and Bree Harper appears wearing only an oversized shirt, the tails hanging just below the tops of her thighs. Her bare legs are taut and muscled, yet still feminine and soft. There is something different about her now, an animalistic quality. Sleek but powerful, she slides up against Nikki and wraps her arms around her waist. Nikki tosses her head back so their cheeks touch, and Bree playfully nuzzles her neck.

The tightness in Dignon's crotch increases.

Bree cups Nikki's breasts, and Nikki turns so they're facing each other.

They kiss passionately, hungrily.

With a quick and violent tug of Nikki's hair, her head twists at an unnatural angle and her neck appears to snap. Her body goes limp and collapses to the floor, out of sight.

Bree's mouth opens and twists as if she's in sudden agony. Her eyes roll to solid black, her face shifts and changes, the bones and structure impossibly stretching and elongated as she morphs into some alternate creature.

Dignon jumps back, away from the window and stares straight ahead a moment, uncertain if he's seen what he thinks he has.

But Bree is gone.

The room is empty.

The light goes out.

His vision adjusts to the darkness, focuses on the night.

It has stopped snowing.

Blood In Electric Blue

There is movement behind him, in the bathroom doorway. He looks back, expecting to see Mr. Tibbs.

It is Bree Harper instead.

Something between a groan and a strangled scream of shock and terror escapes him, most of it dying in his throat. He staggers back, loses his balance, his feet slipping on—water? A rush of seawater, beach sand and seaweed floating in it, gushes across his bathroom floor. He reaches for a towel bar to prevent his fall but crashes against the wall before managing to steady himself.

"Don't be afraid." Bree's violet eyes, wide and intense, cut the shadows. Her face has returned to normal. "Do you know how long I've searched for you? Years, Dignon, decades. *Centuries.*"

Pain shoots up through his temple and settles behind his eyes. He brings a trembling hand to his cheek. His flesh is warm and clammy.

"Don't you know how special you are?" she asks. "Do you have any idea the things you're capable of, the power you possess?"

"I dreamed of you, a nightmare, I—"

"It wasn't a dream, Dignon, it wasn't a nightmare."

According to legend, they are often sought after, enslaved or destroyed by a myriad of evil beings or practitioners of black magic who seek to draw power by possessing the darkness engulfing a Death Maker's soul.

A violent tremor throttles him from head to toe. Nausea grips him. He tries to speak but cannot.

Bree slowly unbuttons her shirt. "Come closer."

A painful tightness clamps across Dignon's chest like a vise, and his knees buckle. He slides to the floor, barely able to breathe.

She opens her mouth, her lips parting slowly as she lets the shirt slide back over her shoulders and fall to the floor at her bare feet.

Greg F. Gifune

What Dignon hears is inhuman; a sound captivating and grotesque, an otherworldly shriek that mesmerizes and shreds his soul at once. What Dignon sees sends him tumbling into unconsciousness, blinded by the brilliance of her beauty, his eyes burned to sightless raw orbs from staring directly into the magnificence of the sun.

* * *

As light flickers through the darkness, his vision returns, and with it, terror.

The world appears at an angle. He realizes he's lying on his stomach, the bathroom tile dry but cool against his flushed cheek. It's morning, but at some point during the night he's fallen from the toilet.

His fear retreats. Confusion steps in.

Lightheaded, Dignon struggles to his feet. He feels like he's been pummeled from head to toe. In the mirror he discovers a bruise below his left eye, the puffy blotch of purple, yellow and black a testament to the force with which his face hit the floor. He presses on it. Pain pulses across his face. Odd, he thinks, how beauty always appears when he least expects it. He watches the bruise a while, unable to take his eyes from it.

In time, he plucks the empty beer bottle from the sink, puts it aside then runs the water. Cupping a small amount in his hands, he splashes it across his face. The jarring temperature awakens him fully. He cups another handful and this time drinks it, which soothes his dry-mouth but does little to combat his horribly sour breath. Brushing his teeth solves the problem, but once he's finished he finds himself standing over the sink, bent at the waist and studying the water with great fascination as it swirls and gurgles down the small drain. Dignon wonders what it looks like down there, deep in the pipes amidst the rust and sludge and slime. Were a person trapped somewhere down there, would he know? Would anyone? Could he hear them? Could they hear him?

The Band-Aid on his finger has become worn and soiled. He carefully peels it back, the glue adhering to and pulling his skin. He finds specks of blood staining the small netting in the center of the Band-Aid's underbelly, so he tosses the bandage into the trash. After retrieving a fresh one from the medicine cabinet, he applies it to his finger, hiding the circular raw area that has turned a bizarre shade of pink since the last time he saw it. This layer of him, this part of his flesh designed to remain hidden, looks like a burst blister, the dead skin torn away. Dignon tightens the Band-Aid. His fingertip throbs in response a few times then falls quiet.

Mr. Tibbs appears in the doorway. Perhaps he's been there all along.

He gazes deep into the cat's eyes, searching for something — anything — that might deliver him from this.

With a sigh, Mr. Tibbs saunters off down the hallway.

Dignon moves to the window. The storm has finally ceased but the glass is caked with ice and a swathe of snow that's been blown across the lower portion of the pane like sand art. With a hand towel, he wipes condensation from the window until the building next door comes into view.

Nikki's shade is drawn.

ELEVEN

He sits in front of the window overlooking the street and drinks his coffee, waiting and watching, confident that sooner or later Nikki will emerge from her apartment. The snow has stopped and the city has descended into a deep freeze. Even the occasional walker is absent, nothing moves out there, and though Dignon can hear the rumble of nearby snowplows he has yet to actually see one. Dressed in jeans, winter boots and a heavy sweater, a knit hat on his head, he gently strokes the parka in his lap with his free hand. He wants to be ready to spring into action the moment he sees Nikki. She has to be all right, he tells himself, she has to be.

It's Sunday. She's probably sleeping late. It's her day off, isn't it? Must be.

Sunday. The word repeats over and over in Dignon's head. Sunday. Church day when he and Willie were children. They never attended, but their father did, or at least that's where he claimed he went every Sunday morning. And while he was gone, presumably seeking absolution for his sins, his sons suffered for them.

As always, Dignon fights the memories, but they're

Blood In Electric Blue

stronger than usual, more powerful this time, clinging to him and refusing to let go. He begins to perspire.

He remembers that cellar well, the low ceiling, the cement floor cool and slightly damp beneath his bare feet. But most of all he remembers the section directly under the kitchen, where full basement turned to crawl-space and where cement turned to dirt.

Dignon remembers their cat Homer sitting outside in the grass, looking down at them through the narrow cellar window with such soulful eyes.

I'm sorry, he seems to say, *I'd save you if I could.*

"Homer was sent to us by God," Willie says dreamily, drifting in and out of consciousness. "All you have to do is look into his eyes to know that. All the mysteries of the universe are locked away in those eyes, only no one sees, no one understands."

"How can you still believe in God?"

"How can you not?"

Willie's face is so very pale, eyes closed but moving rapidly beneath the lids, the only indication of life. "Tell me a story," Willie says, slurring the words. "Tell me a story Dignon."

"What kind of story?"

"Anything, a—an adventure or a love story or a fantasy, anything at all."

A slight breeze moves through the crawlspace, seeping through the cracks and spaces in the molding and the aging wood frame, the paint around the tiny window cracked and flaked. Dignon detects the faint aroma of food. Cooking, someone is cooking—grilling— some distance away, the delicious smells carried on the wind only to die in this awful place. Music...can he hear music too?

And then, panic. Eyes opening to the pipes and network of cobwebs just inches from his face, the dirt beneath him somehow loose and hard all at once, the smell of earth mixed with bleach from the washer on the far side of the basement, his body wiggling, trying to move, to escape this confined space, this coffin, this tomb. His body bucks as if in seizure but his attempts at movement are futile. *Get me out get me out please get me out I can't move I can't breathe I can't take it please get me out of here I can't move I can't move I —*

Ironically, movement is what rescues him, returns him to the steaming mug of coffee in his hand, the alleged safety of his apartment, the window before him, the snow and ice and the street below.

The mug in his hand jiggles wildly, nearly spilling his coffee. Carefully, he puts the mug down and clenches his fists until the trembling passes. "Breathe," he whispers. "Breathe."

Through the window, he notices a trash bag down by the curb and focuses his attention on it until the memories have left him. This isn't trash day, why — who would throw a bag of trash there? The bag is in pristine condition and isn't buried under snow, which means it's only been placed there recently.

He studies it more closely.

It begins to move. Rather, something *inside* it begins to move, bowing and violently tenting the plastic in various directions.

Dignon scrambles into his parka and runs for the door.

As he bounds down the front steps toward the curb, his feet slip out from under him and he falls, his body rolling through the snow and sliding along the ice until it finally comes to a stop just shy of the street.

He lays there a moment, flat on his back and out of breath, the dull gray sky stretched out above him. His heart thuds in his chest. With considerable effort, Dignon

Blood In Electric Blue

gets to his hands and knees. A sharp pain rockets across the small of his back but quickly dissipates. Otherwise he seems to be all right. He brushes snow from his trousers and parka then looks around self-consciously. No one has seen, no one has noticed. No one cares.

Suddenly remembering why he was running in the first place, Dignon closes on the trash bag, kneels down and tears it open.

Papers...rotting food...flyers and discarded mail... coffee grounds...

He stares into the trash. His eyes tear, perhaps from the cold. Somewhere deep inside, he can feel himself unraveling.

"Hey."

Standing in the middle of the street in a hooded jacket is Nikki, her usual huge black purse with the skull and crossbones slung over her shoulder. Sans the giant boots, she instead wears clunky black lace-up shoes. Her eyes blink questioningly from inside the hood, the spider makeup encircling them intact but smudged, like she's slept in it.

"Hi," he says dully.

"What are you doing?"

"Just...I don't know, I..." He motions to the trash.

"Did somebody dump that there?"

"Yeah, I was just about to pick it up."

Nikki finishes crossing the street, stands over him and what remains of the trash bag. "Unbelievable." She bends over and attempts to close the tear. "I'll help you."

Together, they carry the bag and its contents to the alley between their buildings and dispose of it in one of the trash cans there. Dignon catches a whiff of cigarettes and body odor wafting from her. "Can I ask you a question?" he says, wiping his hands on his parka.

She shrugs. "OK."

"Were you home last night?"

"Dude, does it look like I was home last night? I'm just getting home now. Couldn't even get a cab 'cause of this snow, had to walk my ass here in the cold." She sniffles then paws at her nose with the back of her hand. "Why?"

"No reason, I..." He tries desperately to think of something to say. "Mrs. Rogo's apartment's been dark since yesterday. I was wondering if maybe you knew where she went."

Nikki looks to the apartment window. "Maybe she went to go visit that snotty daughter of hers. You know the one with the rug-rats?"

"Yeah that's probably it." Visions from the night before flood his head. "Nikki, do you know anyone named Bree Harper?"

"Name's not ringing a bell. Should it?"

"She's a friend of mine. I thought I saw you with her once."

"I tend to be *really* sociable, know what I mean?" She smiles playfully. "Maybe I forgot her name. It happens."

He stands there, freezing and unable to think of a response.

"Hey, you should've seen the shit over by Borges Lane," Nikki says.

Bree, he thinks. "Borges Lane?"

"Yeah, I partied with this chick who lives near there last night, ended up crashing at her place. Anyway, I'm walking through there on the way home, right? And the whole city's locked down from the storm, all quiet and eerie and shit — except for those fucking smokestacks of course — and I see flashing lights and all this commotion over on Borges. Fire trucks, an ambulance, cops everywhere, real circus. Some guy threw himself off a roof last night. Guess nobody saw it or knew and he died and got buried in the snow. One of the plows found the body this morning, ran right over it."

Kyle. He knows it's him.

"Jesus," Dignon mutters.

"Personally, if I was gonna do myself I'd take pills or something. I don't think I'd have the balls to jump off a roof."

Doesn't make any difference now, it's already over for me.

Grasping at straws he says, "Well, I'm glad you're OK."

"Why wouldn't I be?" When Dignon looks down awkwardly at the sidewalk rather than answer, she responds with an unexpected smile. "You wanna come up and have some coffee with me?"

"Coffee?"

"Yeah, it's a beverage."

"You mean now?"

"No, a week from next Tuesday at noon," she says with a roll of her eyes. "Whatever, it's freezing out here, I just thought—"

"Yes."

"Yes?"

"Yes, I'd like to come up and have some coffee with you." He clears his throat and attempts a smile. "Thank you."

She stares at him like he's spoken a language she can't quite comprehend. After a moment, she cocks her head toward her building. "Come on then."

*   *   *

The apartment is small, surprisingly neat and well organized, but decorated in apparent tribute to an earlier era. A huge framed poster dominates the main wall of the living room, a reproduction of The Sex Pistols album,

Greg F. Gifune

black letters on a pink background that reads: *Never Mind the Bollocks Here's the Sex Pistols,* and though the room is sparsely furnished, what's there is dated and stylistically pure middle to late 1970s. From the bead curtains hanging in the doorways to the lava lamp on the coffee table, to the television (a small set with rabbit ears sitting on a cart), to the stereo (an all-in-one 8-track, turntable and FM tuner), the speakers mounted on shelves built into the wall amidst framed movie posters and a neon bar sign advertising Cold Duck sparkling wine, everything is retro. Dignon sits on a stiff inexpensive couch and takes it all in, awaiting his coffee and Nikki's return from the kitchen.

He knows she's lived here quite a while, but there's something strange about the feel of this apartment. It seems staged, forced somehow, like it's been constructed with the sole purpose of convincing him she lives here and regularly inhabits this space as her own. In the past, when he's tried to imagine what her apartment might look like, the picture that forms in his mind has been similar to this, but there's no true sense of Nikki as a grown woman here. It strikes him as more a set than actual living quarters, a concept piece conjured in the mind of a rebellious teenage girl attempting to find her way, her own sense of style and expression in 1970-something. Or perhaps it's just someone else's idea of what it might look like. Maybe that's it, he thinks, maybe it's not about who she really is but rather how others see and interpret her. Maybe that's what Nikki's life has become, the constant portrayal of a dreary character in someone else's play.

Dignon cranes his neck in an attempt to see down the narrow hallway off the living room. Surely it leads to the room he's able to see from the bathroom of his own apartment, but from his position on the couch it remains

155

beyond reach.

Moving through a curtain of clicking and swaying beads, Nikki enters the living room carrying matching glass cups brimming with hot coffee. "It's instant," she announces, handing him one. "My Mr. Coffee shit the bed a couple days ago."

Dignon notices that since she disappeared into the kitchen, she has removed her coat, shoes and socks, and now wears a pair of battered jeans and a gray sleeveless sweatshirt that reads: *University of Go-Fuck-Yourself.* Several dark tattoos decorate her arms, and her multi-colored shock of hair is mussed and limp rather than in its usual spiked state. She lowers herself into a big square chair that looks like it might've been part of a sectional at one point, and tucks her legs beneath her. Her toes are painted with the same black polish adorning her fingernails. "Thanks," he says, holding up the cup for emphasis before taking a sip. The coffee is harsh, stronger than he's used to.

"What happened to your finger?" Nikki asks, motioning to his hand.

Dignon considers it a moment. The Band-Aid still looks fresh. "I don't know."

"You don't know?"

"A blister, I guess," he tells her. "Top must've fallen off, it's all raw skin. I keep putting a Band-Aid on it but it doesn't seem to heal." To buy time, Dignon drinks more coffee.

"So what do you do, anyway?" she asks.

"I'm on disability at the moment."

"What are you mental or something?"

He feels himself blush. "I have some issues I'm working out."

"Shit, get in line. Hope you at least get some decent drugs out of the deal."

Dignon smiles clumsily. "You work over at that club, right?"

"Yeah, *Couplings*. Ever been?"

"No. I've been by it, though, my sister lives near there."

"It's supposed to be a couples club for swingers but mostly it's just a bunch of horny losers sipping overpriced drinks and looking to get their cocks sucked on."

"What do you do there?"

"I bartend." She sips her coffee. "Usually topless."

Dignon does his best to maintain a neutral expression. "Cool."

She lets out a bark of laughter that quickly turns into a cough. Nikki remedies this by lighting a cigarette. "You're all right, Darby."

"It's, um, Dignon."

"Oops."

"No problem, it's an unusual name."

"True. I mean, no offense, but what the hell were your parents thinking?"

"It was my grandfather's name, my mother's father," he explains. "She wanted his name to live on, so she gave it to me."

"Great, thanks Mom." She takes a deep drag on her cigarette, throws her head back and blasts a stream of smoke at the ceiling. "Anyway, sorry, we've been neighbors since, like, forever, I should know your name by now."

"Are you from here originally?"

"Dude, nobody's from here originally. My family moved to Pennsylvania years ago, but I was born and raised in a little town about half an hour from here."

Dignon hesitates, the steaming coffee just shy of his lips. He lowers the cup. Though he's tempted to ask the name of her hometown, he doesn't. He's not sure why.

Blood In Electric Blue

Instead he says, "Me too."

"Gotta love those small towns," Nikki scoffs. "I couldn't get out of mine fast enough. First chance I got after I hit eighteen, I booked it. Went out to L.A. for a while but it didn't work out, ended up here. What are you gonna do, right? Everybody's got to end up somewhere."

Dignon scans the wall, studies the movie posters.

"I'm kind of a movie freak," she confesses. "You like movies?"

"I like old movies the best. I wasn't supposed to but I used to stay up late and watch them when I was little. There was a show on one of the old UHF channels that showed classics every Saturday night at ten and then at midnight they'd switch to old B sci-fi and horror movies like *Hercules Against the Moon Men.*"

"Shut *up!*" She slaps the cushion next to her. "I used to watch that channel! This dude with a bad rug and a cheesy tuxedo used to introduce them, right?"

"That's the one." Dignon settles on one movie poster in particular. It features an array of colors displayed as a series of small dots arranged into patterns that form a man's face at the top of the poster and a woman's at the bottom. Both faces appear troubled.

"Alphaville," Nikki says. "Jean-Luc Godard."

He shakes his head.

"Foreign film, really good. The little art theater over by the club shows it now and then. I know an usher there. He let me have one of the posters last time they were showing it." Nikki adjusts her position in the chair so she can see the poster too. "It's about this intergalactic secret agent that goes to this city on another planet where a huge fascist computer runs everything. It's like an Orwellian thing where everyone's given up their rights to the government and nobody gives a shit about anything. Everybody's like all mindless and shit, and they have tons of sex but none of it means anything because people aren't allowed to have emotions. If they show emotion the computer kills them."

Dignon can almost hear his father scolding Willie for exhibiting emotion.

Don't be such a goddamn sissy.

"No emotion," he mumbles.

"Not even love."

Daddy, don't.

"We've all had sex without love, right?" Before Dignon can answer she says, "But it's like the lottery or going to Vegas or something. You know you probably won't win and that the odds are against you, only you don't give a shit because there's that chance, that one chance that maybe you'll get lucky and hit it. Maybe one of these times it won't just be sex. It'll be love." She takes a drag from her cigarette and exhales through her nose. "But in Alphaville there's not even a chance. The way things are going, Godard probably had it right. They're already trying to outlaw free thought, emotions can't be that far behind. Imagine if we could only cry or laugh or feel if the government gave us permission?"

"Who wins?" Dignon asks.

'What do you mean?"

"In the movie, who wins?"

Nikki lowers her eyes, drinks some coffee. "Nobody wins."

A gust of wind slams the building.

"Sometimes I feel like Lemmy Caution," she says, and then, realizing he has no idea who that is, explains, "The guy in Alphaville, the secret agent. I feel like I'm from somewhere else — maybe The Outlands, like him — and I'm stuck in the middle of this fucked up city where nothing makes sense and where nothing's real or what it appears to be because what it and we were meant to be is so long gone maybe it never even was, you know what I'm saying? Like we're under the control of something bigger and just sleepwalking through time, marking the days until we get answers, some clue as to what the hell it's all about."

Dignon swallows coffee, hopeful she'll continue. He's never even thought about Nikki in any meaningful context. She's always been the oddball woman next door with the crazy hair and the wild outfits, and suddenly, she has revealed herself to be a fully formed human being with intelligence and emotion, with soul. Had he really expected anything less? He's always instinctually recognized the aura of loneliness just beneath her flamboyant guise, and maybe that's why he's been fascinated by her, why he's felt a kinship of sorts to her, albeit from a distance. Now, with the opportunity to see her as she truly is, Dignon realizes she possesses many of the same subtle looks or awkward mannerisms he sometimes catches himself displaying, tells that signal uneasiness in her own skin, discomfort with her own existence. It is pain not from outside but from within, an affliction managed though never quite cured. "'What is the privilege of the dead?'" she asks, quoting Alphaville. "'To die no more.' How cool is that?"

"Maybe it's all a myth," he suggests.

"Life's too painful to be a fable. Nice thought, though."

His fingertip is sore beneath the Band-Aid. Dignon presses it against the side of the coffee mug until he feels warmth and the ache subsides. "I don't know," he says. "Some fables are awfully brutal. Remember the fairy tales from when we were kids?"

"I try not to." She shakes her head and runs a hand through her hair, fluffing it with her fingers. "When I lived at home my life was so boring and nowhere, I mean, I used to sit around trying to dream shit up just to make it interesting, you know? What kind of life is it if you have to constantly do things to remind yourself you're still alive?"

The wind whips across the building again, its ferocity gaining momentum.

"We lived in this little house on a quiet rural street," Nikki says, looking at the window over Dignon's shoulder, her painted and smudged eyes reflecting a sudden distance. "We only had two neighbors and there was a lot of space between the houses, a couple acres or more, so it was kind of like not having neighbors at all. My bedroom was upstairs and faced the street. When I was in high school I used to get undressed in front of the window just for kicks and to see how it would feel and what might happen, you know? I did it probably twenty times, and you know what? Nobody ever noticed. There wasn't a lot of traffic on the street since it was so out of the way, but even now and then when a car would go by, they didn't see me. I'd stand there naked in front of that window with the light on for hours, just thinking. The house was quiet, nothing moving outside, nobody around but a sky full of stars, and I'd convince myself that maybe somewhere—maybe even in one of those houses—somebody was watching, somebody could see. And when I pretended they could that's when I felt it. That's when I felt alive." A tense smile twitches across her face. "And then one day, a car did stop. It drove by at first, but the brake lights came on really fast and the car backed up and pulled over right in front of the house. It was really late, my parents were asleep and except for my room the house was dark. But the driver, he shut his car lights off anyway. He must've been lost or something— who knows—but nobody came down that road unless

Blood In Electric Blue

they meant to or took a wrong turn. Still, it was so weird, for the first time I didn't have to wonder if someone could see me, someone way off in the distance. Whoever was in that car had seen me, *was* seeing me, and whoever he was, he needed to watch just like I needed to show him. Shit, I was seventeen years old and standing in the light while some guy I didn't know and couldn't see looked at me. I didn't do anything, I just stood there. A couple minutes later the headlights came back on and the car drove off. I never saw it again, but even after it left, I stayed in the window for some reason. I always figured when it happened—when I knew for sure—it'd be the most erotic thing ever. It wasn't. I was turned on a little but it was more than that. There was something spiritual about it, and after a while the night changed. It was liquid, you know? Washing over me and moving inside me like blood, keeping me alive and connected to…something." She puts the remains of her coffee aside then takes a final pull on her cigarette and butts it in a plastic ashtray. "When I was alone again and had to wonder if anyone was watching, it all started to make sense. There *was* somebody out there, I was sure of it, somebody who saw me. *Me.* It wasn't dirty at all. There was beauty to it, purity we couldn't quite touch, but it was out there swimming in that night sky between us. And it mattered. I could feel it. It mattered."

Dignon closes his eyes. A pinhole of light emerges from the darkness, slowly grows brighter, stronger, and eventually becomes Nikki standing in a window.

"Did that story disturb you?" she asks.

"No."

"Did it turn you on?"

"No."

"What then?"

"It made me feel like I know you." He opens his eyes,

finds her sitting across from him. "It made me feel like I understand."

"And do you? Do you understand?"

"Yes, I think so."

Nikki weighs this a while. "I've never told anyone about that before."

"Why did you tell me?"

"I don't know."

"I'm flattered you did."

"Tell me something now. Something you've never told anyone before."

After considerable silence he says, "I'm ashamed."

"Of what?"

"Everything."

Nikki swings her feet around to the floor. "Do you want to fuck me, Dignon?"

He stares at her, hapless. "What?"

"Do you want to fuck me?"

The wind howls, as if in rescue, and the building shakes and creaks against the onslaught. Somewhere far off but woven within the wind is something else, something more. Dignon stands, looks to the window. "Do you hear that?"

"The wind? Of course."

"No, listen. Inside the wind, can you hear it?"

Nikki frowns. "*Inside* the wind?"

Have you heard it yet?

"It's her," he mutters.

"Who?"

"I have to go."

Nikki stands, moves toward him then hesitates. "Look, I didn't mean to freak you out, OK? We can just hang out and play some records if you want. I was feeling vulnerable or whatever and there was this connection and I…"

Blood In Electric Blue

He looks back at her.

"Jesus, are you all right?"

"No."

She puts her hands in her pockets and rocks back on her heels like a nervous teenager. "Do you want to stay?"

"Yes," he whispers. In his mind he can see her in that window again, nude and alone. But she's not alone. She never was. He's there too. "But I can't."

Nikki's shoulders droop and her posture weakens, like she's lost all the air in her body. Her hands fall free of her pockets and dangle lifelessly at her sides. The black smudges around her eyes, once spiders, no longer look intimidating or tough. They're just peculiar and sad, a failed attempt to shield and conceal her from all the things that have stalked and cornered her on this cold winter day. "Then get out," she tells him.

The wind dies and he finds himself reaching for her. "I'm sorry, I—"

"Go on, get out."

"Nikki, I know what it's like to—"

"Get the fuck out!"

Her scream freezes him, sends him hurtling back to that dark and terrifying crawlspace where she is a specter behind distant glass, a ghost well beyond his grasp. As she always was. As she always will be.

TWELVE

The phone in his apartment is ringing, as he knew it would be. Having sprinted up the stairs to answer it in time, he is out of breath once he stumbles into the kitchen and snatches the phone from the wall. "Yes?"

"Dig?"

Willie, not Bree. His heart plummets. He recognizes the tone of her voice, knows it too well.

Help me, Dig. Help me.

"What's wrong?"

"Can you come over? I..."

"Tell me what's wrong."

Something brushes the phone, causing a scraping sound in the connection. "I really need to see you," she says, blowing her nose a moment later. "Please, love. Please."

"I'm on my way."

The line disconnects, becomes a dial tone. Dignon remains in place, the phone to his ear, his hand clutching it so tightly his entire arm shakes.

Mrs. Rogo still isn't home. The Christmas tree in her window remains dark. No cooking smells, no Christmas

Blood In Electric Blue

carols, no sounds of movement or life in her apartment below. She's even taken in the silly ceramic Santa Claus on the front steps. Dignon has never before realized how comforting these things are to him. Where have she and Schnitzel gone? The wind cries, summons him. Or is it only the cruel taunts of banshees again, hidden beneath ice and snow?

In his mind, day becomes night and it is snowing again. From the top of the roof, through a haze of flakes, he sees the factory stacks spill smoke into the sky above the city. At the edge of the roof is Kyle, head bowed and hands covering his ears, his unbuttoned coat flapping in the wind. He does not look back before he steps out into space. Initially it seems the air will hold and allow him to float from rooftop to rooftop like some miraculous creature undetected in the dead of night. But then he pitches forward, his hands leave his ears and snap out on either side of him, and he plummets into the swirling snow.

As he freefalls, Dignon imagines Kyle thinking about his mother, his father, perhaps siblings, a wife and the children he'll never have, the life he'll never know. But he's sure that what Kyle thinks about most is time. Ironically, he has an endless supply of it now, beneath this perfect moonlight. And in the seconds before body meets ground, Kyle is filled neither with terror nor regret. Instead it is beauty he feels, beauty he sees. Undeniable, infinite beauty.

Kyle dies alone in the snow and cold, but Dignon will remember it differently. He will remember only a silent fall through darkness, a sky full of snowflakes and the grandeur of it all.

The pain in his palm where the phone digs into his flesh reminds Dignon that like Kyle, the night has come and gone.

Greg F. Gifune

He sees Mr. Tibbs sitting nearby watching him, and finally loosens his grip and replaces the phone in its cradle. The cat holds his gaze for several moments, calms, centers, and brings him back.

I'm sorry.

"I know, Tibbs. I know."

I'd save you if I could.

Dignon goes to him, pets his head and neck and shoulders, embraces and kisses him again and again. The cat leans into him approvingly, adoringly, and begins to purr. "You're my best friend," Dignon whispers. "And I love you."

Eyes brimming with tears, he grabs something from a kitchen drawer then leaves without looking back, unsure if he will ever see Mr. Tibbs again.

*   *   *

He knocks but no one answers, so he tries the door. It's unlocked.

The apartment is a mess. Wilma's dressing table has been tipped over and her various trays of makeup, costume jewelry and other accessories lie scattered across the floor. A hole has been punched into the poster of Marlene Dietrich, the stereo has been ripped from the wall and smashed to pieces, and the Christmas tree has fallen to its side, a few ornaments crushed and littering the red felt skirting around its base. The lone package beneath the tree, the box Dignon wrapped himself, looks as if it's been stomped numerous times. The top is caved in and the paper torn. Her array of wigs has been knocked to the floor as well, many of them ruined. The kitchenette area and the bed against the far wall are the only things intact and apparently untouched.

Wilma sits on the floor in nothing but a short silk robe

Blood In Electric Blue

that barely covers her, a phone she has pulled from the nightstand next to her, the cord running back across the bare floor like an umbilical tethering her to some other place and time. Her head hangs down and her hands are positioned out on either side of her, propping her upright. Spent tissues litter the floor around her. For some reason a nearby window is open, the curtains fluttering gracefully as occasional bursts of loose snow on the sill blow into the apartment and accumulate in a pile a few feet away.

The apartment is freezing. Dignon watches his breath take flight then looks to the bed. Barry lies atop the ruffled covers, unconscious or asleep, he can't be sure which.

Wilma sees her brother, raises eyes smeared with makeup and tears, mascara running down her cheeks in long black stains like wounds. Next to her right eye is a small cut, some bruising and swelling, and her bottom lip is caked with dried blood. A crooked brunette wig sits atop her head. Self-consciously, she reaches up and straightens it. She looks like a child, Dignon thinks, like a lost child from long ago, confused and frightened and broken.

Dignon closes the door behind him, then goes to the window and slides it shut. Without comment he moves to the thermostat on the wall, turns it up then stands over the bed. On the nightstand is a burnt spoon, a syringe and a spent book of matches. He pulls a comforter from the foot of the bed, places it over Wilma and wraps her in it. She accepts it but says nothing as Dignon returns to the bed, his hands buried in his coat pockets.

Barry's long, thin, hairless body reminds Dignon of an insect. But for a pair of bikini-style briefs, he is nude. His suit, shirt, socks and long leather coat clutter a nearby chair. Dignon watches his narrow chest rise and fall. Oddly, Barry's curly-perm looks perfect as ever.

Dignon studies him a while.

Eventually Barry's eyes blink open. His mouth moves as he licks his lips and makes what sound like chewing noises, coughs and then realizes who it is standing over the bed. His expression is at first one of confusion, but quickly turns to annoyance. With a sniffle, he sits up. "What're you doing here?"

Dignon says nothing.

"Oh." Barry swallows, coughs again then puts his feet on the floor. He notices the state of the apartment, and though Wilma's back is to him, he sees her too. "Yeah, things got a little out of hand last night." He glances at the nightstand but makes no mention of the syringe, spoon or used matchbook. "Why is it so cold in here?"

Only the wind bothers to answer.

His face contorts as he yawns dramatically. Old acne scars on his cheeks are more pronounced at close range. "Nothing personal, Dig-man, but waking up and finding you standing over the bed staring at me qualifies as big-time creepy."

Dignon stares at him.

"OK, listen up because I'm only saying this once." With a bored sigh, Barry stands and rubs his eyes. He is much taller than Dignon. "All this," he says, motioning to the rest of the apartment, "is between Willie and me. It's our business, nobody else's. I don't explain myself to anybody. But because I like you, I'll tell you this much. Willie got out of line and disrespected me, so she gets what she gets. It's that simple."

Dignon steps closer.

"Don't try to be a hero," Barry says. "You're not cut out for it, babe. Christ, look at you, man. What are you gonna do, *fight* me?"

Blood In Electric Blue

"Save me," Dignon says just above a whisper.

Barry cocks an eyebrow. "What?"

"Save me," he says, voice strangled with emotion. "Save *us*."

"What the hell are you talking about?"

"Isn't it easier to save us? Isn't it easier than hurting us?"

Barry backs away uneasily, grabs his clothes from the chair and hurriedly begins to dress, eyes on Dignon throughout. "Goddamn freaks, the two of you."

"Why would you choose cruelty? Why would you do that?"

"OK, I get it. This is some reverse psychology, pacifist bullshit, am I right?"

"No. You're not."

Fully dressed, Barry grabs his coat from the chair and slinks into it. "The world's a brutal place, Dig-man. You and Willie go through life like two little kids cowering in a corner. That's your problem. It's pathetic. Try growing a set."

Dignon removes one hand from his coat pocket and holds it down against the side of his leg. "Have you ever been in that corner, Barry?"

He tries to see what Dignon's holding in his hand. "What've you got there?"

"Do you know what I am?"

"A pain in my ass?"

"Thanatos Kataskevastis."

"Gesundheit."

"It's Greek. The earliest traces of my kind were found in Ancient Greece."

"Your kind?"

"Death Makers."

The hammer hits Barry in the cheek, making a strange clanking sound as it connects with bone. His head snaps back and to the side, and with a look of puzzlement and shock, he staggers back, shakes his head then touches his face as if to be certain it's still intact. It isn't.

Swinging with a long arcing motion, Dignon hits him again, this time on the other side of his face. On the backswing he connects with Barry's chin, the third blow sending him into the nightstand. The lamp crashes to the floor and Barry clutches his face with both hands, hits the wall with his shoulder then collapses.

"'Though melancholy and nonviolent by nature," Dignon mumbles, stepping over pieces of lamp and raising the hammer again, "given the right conditions these beings can also be consciously dangerous and extremely volatile.'"

Barry says something unintelligible and dizzily reaches for the nightstand just before Dignon slams the hammer down across his forearm, shattering bone with an audible crack. Barry releases a rasping groan from deep within him as he clutches his arm, flops onto his side and curls into a fetal position, dark bruising already forming across his jaw-line and cheeks.

Dignon straddles him, envisions smashing Barry's skull to a frothy pulp.

With strangely beautiful rhythm, he swings the hammer back and forth, striking Barry again and again with what soon becomes a wet, squishing sound. Blood sprays Dignon's face and neck, but he continues to swing, methodically, purposefully, back and forth, back and forth. It feels wonderful.

"Don't kill him." Wilma's voice sounds miles away.

He blinks away blood and slides the hammer back into his coat pocket. Dignon watches his victim's fallen form a moment and what he has done begins to sink in. Trembling, he backs away.

Blood In Electric Blue

"Is he dead?" Wilma asks.

Dignon looks back at her. She's still sitting on the floor staring into space.

"*Is he dead?*"

"I think so."

Though there's not much to him, Barry at deadweight is surprisingly heavy. Lifting him under the arms, Dignon somehow manages to get him back to the bed without falling himself. Barry flops onto the mattress, a boneless doll, discarded and bloody. The bruising along his jaw and cheeks has already gotten worse, the damage apparent, and blood leaks from the corner of his mouth and various wounds across his face and head. Dignon looks to the window as he catches his breath.

The neighborhood out there is little more than a frozen ghost town. Out there. The words repeat in his head. Out there.

The smells…the sounds…the memories…the screams… his father's face…

Dignon sits on the floor next to Wilma. He feels himself crumbling to pieces from a place so deep inside that he's unable to stop it. Like the blood flowing through his veins, he has no jurisdiction there and is powerless to control it.

"I'm so cold," he says. "Willie, I'm so cold."

"Sometimes it's good to be cold. It reminds us we're still alive."

As she turns and looks at him, with her bruises and cuts, Dignon begins to weep. "I'm sorry. Christ, I'm so sorry, I'm sorry, I'm so sorry."

"For what, love?"

"I can't make it, Willie. I can't do it."

"It's all right. Really, it is."

"I don't know what to do anymore. I don't think I ever did."

"Close your eyes and live your life, Dig. Live your life."

"There's no life left."

"Then lay your head down here with me and rest."

Wiping the tears from his eyes, he places his face in her lap. The wind calls him, but he tries instead to focus on the gentle motion of Wilma's fingers tenderly rubbing the back of his head. "Are we dead Willie? Have we died?"

"We're just lost," she whispers. "Lost in the dark a while."

"I can't stay here. I have to go."

"Then go, love. Go."

Dignon lets the darkness embrace him with what he can only hope is escape, perhaps even peace.

But no one is ever really alone, especially in the dark.

*   *   *

Black becomes white. Everything is shrouded in ice, the snow sprinkled with diamond dust. The sun burns strong in an otherwise dull winter sky, gilding the city, bathing it in white gold.

Amidst the serenity, the old abandoned tenement.

Dignon finds himself sitting in the company van parked just outside, Jackie Shine next to him behind the wheel, a toothpick tucked into the corner of his mouth. A breath-cloud slowly rises toward the roof. Dignon looks closer. The same James Dean hair, the barracuda jacket with the collar up, the squinty but intense eyes, it's definitely him. "Jackie?"

A quick sideways glance and then, "How's it going, kid?"

Dignon knows he should be frightened, but he's not. He feels relieved, safe. "What are you doing here?"

Blood In Electric Blue

"Just dropping you off is all."

Dignon looks through the icy van window to the tenement and his feelings of safety evaporate. "I don't want to go in there."

"Can't blame you on that one."

A dim yellow light fills a window facing the street. "But I have to, don't I."

"Afraid so."

A shadow moves behind old, tattered curtains. "Will I ever come out?"

Jackie Shine runs a hand up over his forehead and nods. "Yeah, you'll come out." The steam of his breath climbs past his face like mist. "You just won't be the same."

"The same?"

"It changes you. That's what life does."

Hot dry air blasts from the vents, hits Dignon's face and reminds him how warm it is in the van. But then...if the heater is on and the windows are rolled up, why can he see his partner's breath?

Dignon drops his eyes to Jackie Shine's lap. The vapor rises not from his mouth or nostrils, but from the bloody gaping wound in his abdomen. Chunks of raw flesh and stringy entrails dangle from the jagged crater, the heat inside his body escaping in a steady rising steam. With a look of horror and astonishment, Dignon brings a hand to his mouth for fear he may vomit.

"Won't heal." Jackie Shine gazes down at it. "It never heals. Why is that?"

Pain pulses in Dignon's fingertip. The Band-Aid has fallen off, revealing the same raw circle of skin that's been there all along. "I was hoping you'd know."

"I've heard stories. People talk. They say sometimes what we imagine is far worse than anything the world can throw at us." Jackie Shine sighs wearily. "Maybe

that's true for some, but not us. Load of crap. Way I see
it, doesn't much matter anyway. Me, I just keep my head
down and drive my van."

"Did I do wrong, Jackie? Have I done some wrong
that's —"

"It's not about right and wrong, kid. Never was." He
fiddles with the toothpick in his mouth, drops the
column shift into drive and revs the engine. "You just
remember what I always told you. Never go out afraid.
Don't give them the fucking satisfaction."

Hand on the door release, Dignon returns his stare to
the tenement. "What's waiting on me in there?"

"Pain and sorrow," he says softly. "Whole lot of pain
and sorrow."

Dignon steps out onto the curb. With a halfhearted
wave, he slam shuts the door and the van pulls away in
a cloud of exhaust, ambling down the otherwise empty
street before turning and disappearing around the corner.

Behind him, the front door of the tenement opens.

"Welcome back."

He recognizes the pompous accent immediately. The
older man in the smoking jacket stands in the doorway, a
mixed drink in one hand and a cigarette in the other. He
smiles with his horse-teeth dentures, his silver hair meticulously combed back, each strand in place, and his
pencil-thin mustache so perfect at first glance it looks as
if it's been drawn on.

I'm always listening, Dignon. Always.

"Come inside," the man says. "We've been expecting
you."

Dignon moves slowly across the sidewalk, up the
tenement steps and follows the man into the foyer. The
door to the apartment is open to reveal shuffling
shadows within, the same as in his nightmare.
Hesitating at the door, the man makes a theatrical

sweeping gesture with his cigarette hand for Dignon to proceed. "After you."

The apartment is not as he remembers it. When he and Jackie Shine had delivered here, but for the sparsest furnishings in the dining area and one of the bedrooms, the apartment was empty. It's now fully furnished with nicely preserved but drab and wildly dated furniture. The sitting room Dignon steps into resembles something from a gloomy Victorian gothic thriller, and houses several people, some sitting on ornate loveseats and high-backed chairs, others standing and milling about. Most have drinks in their hands or are smoking, and though Dignon cannot locate the source, soft classical music plays in the background. Some of the people present are in the middle of what appear to be intense conversations, but they speak under their breath and he cannot make out anything they're saying. Others stare at him with cold, emotionless eyes.

Roy, the policeman from his nightmare stands a few feet away, a mixed drink in his hand despite being in full uniform. Through a derisive grin he chuckles, "What do you say, counselor? Hey, no hard feelings, right?"

Standing next to him is Clarence, his old boss from *Tech Metropolis* in his usual nylon sweat suit and high-top Nikes. Both driving teams from work are there too: Outlaw in full biker regalia, Boo at his side, shaved head shiny and reflecting the dim light; Adam, dapper as ever, and his partner Blondie, her bleached hair wild and harsh, a Pall Mall dangling from her lips. All are gathered in a circle and chatting quietly. They smile and acknowledge Dignon in turn, but he can't be sure if they're complicit in all this or simply pleased to see him.

The man in the smoking jacket closes the door to the apartment behind him and joins another well-dressed man roughly the same age over by a fireplace on the far wall. Dignon recognizes him as the same man who was here the night of the delivery, the one who'd been sitting with the children having dinner. The man in the smoking jacket leans in, whispers something and the other man laughs quietly, watching Dignon with a cruel smirk all the while.

Dignon stands in the center of the room, unsure of what to do.

From the shadows of a doorway leading out of the room and deeper into the apartment, a filthy and disheveled child appears, a young boy of perhaps eight or nine in tattered clothes and no shoes. There is something awry in the boy's face. His eyes, a deep blue and probably once quite striking, are dead and empty, a feature particularly upsetting in one so young. Dignon moves closer to him, unable to break eye contact as a swell of memories rise in him. He sheepishly touches the boy's face, cupping his chin and cheek in his hand. Dignon knows this look. He's seen it before. He's felt it himself. The little boy looks up at him, expression void of emotion. Such things have been thoroughly ripped away from him long ago, and they both know it.

As Dignon battles away tears, he feels a tiny hand slide into his own, and the boy leads him slowly through the doorway along a narrow, sparsely-lit hallway. Other children, some as young as his guide, others a bit older and others still in their early teens, sit on the floor throughout the hallway. Some scratch mindlessly at the walls, others whisper gibberish or simply stare at the floor, helpless, hopeless. All are in need of a bath, better general hygiene and new clothes, yet they seem not to care. Few notice Dignon and the boy at all for that matter, and those who do show little interest in their presence.

At the end of the hallway is a small room. Empty, the

only light comes from a candle encased in a glass globe sitting in the center of the floor, its flame bending flickering ghosts along the walls and ceiling. There are two windows but they've been boarded up from the outside. Beyond them, Dignon can still hear the gusting, crying wind.

The little boy releases his hand and points at the floorboards on the far wall.

Dignon moves closer and sees a small window built into the bottom of the wall. It reminds him of a cellar window, particularly the kind in their home growing up. He shudders and forces a nervous swallow as the boy crouches down, pulls the pane completely out of the window frame and sets it on the floor. From whatever area this small portal leads to, more flickering light seeps free. But this is not candlelight, rather something artificial. Dignon recognizes it immediately as light cast from a television.

After scurrying away, the boy sits with his back against the wall and stares at him, waiting.

With a knot forming in the center of his chest, Dignon carefully takes a knee and peers through the opening.

In the limited light he sees a cramped cement cellar. Someone sits in a wooden chair before a small television placed atop a crate. Though the person's back is to him, he can discern it's male, but little else. To the man's left, an old rusted furnace, silent and broken as the lost souls haunting this horrible testament to depravity and endless suffering. Tension squeezes the back of Dignon's neck, and the raw skin on his fingertip begins to throb and ache.

He looks to the little boy.

The child points to the cellar.

Not certain he can fit through such a small opening, and frightened of what else lies within the little space,

Greg F. Gifune

Dignon squints in an attempt to see more. But the light from the television is insufficient, bathing the man in the chair in quick intervals.

He wants nothing more than to leave here, to grab as many of these poor children as he can and run back out into the snow and cold and scream for help. He knows these feelings of wickedness and unrest all too well, these palpable *things* that hang in the air to create a sensation so disturbing and foul that it leaves one no choice but to do exactly the opposite of what human nature dictates, which is to flee. Because beauty is not alone in its hypnotic qualities. Authentic evil can be even more spellbinding.

Candlelight flickers, mixing with the small patch of light leaking from the opening.

Controlling the fear as best he can, Dignon draws a deep breath, holds it a moment then exhales. With his usual lack of grace, he pushes his head through the window and forces the remainder of his body into the opening, twisting and writhing about like a rodent trapped in the jaws of a snake. Barely managing to fit, he struggles through, and with great effort and a final thrust, slides free and crashes to the cold cement floor. He breaks his fall with his hands and forearms then flops over onto his back, lying breathless like a helpless giant overturned turtle.

It smells musty here, the air dank and stale. The ceiling above him is dark and covered in a thick maze of cobwebs. The floor is cold and bare, the walls rough cement block. Dignon rolls over and up onto all fours, raising his head so he can see the man in the chair and the television on the other side of him.

Even before he regains his feet and moves cautiously around the side of the chair, he knows this is his father. Continuing his slow approach, Dignon looks to the television, and now better able to see the screen, freezes.

He's looking into his own eyes. The scene is a live shot of the cellar, and as he moves and slowly raises an arm, the image does the same. He takes a step back. His TV self steps back as well. Dignon searches the room quickly for either a door or a camera. He finds neither.

"I told you," his father says, voice raspy and exhausted, "once you heard you'd have to act on it, that you wouldn't be able to keep it buried anymore."

Dignon notices feet of barbed wire snugly wrapped around the arms and legs of the chair. It coils up over his father's forearms and calves, holding him in place and forcing him to watch the horror that is his youngest son's life play out on the old black and white television. Trails of dried blood course along his flesh, lead to small circular stains on the floor. His father's face is drawn and pale, the dark bags beneath his eyes thick and heavy, and his receding black hair is mussed and oily and stands up straight in places. His pockmarked skin and wiry build are just as Dignon remembers them, but his once intense eyes are distant, his rage replaced with what he can only hope is regret. Gone is the long coat, the polyester slacks, the lace-up Florsheim shoes, the pressed white shirt and the Timex watch with the fake gold face and cowhide band. Gone is the arrogance and malice, the self-right-eous assuredness of a god with absolute control, able to do whatever he pleases whenever he pleases with no chance of consequence or reciprocation.

His father is nothing, a rotting shell.

"You said I had to go back and find the truth about your death," Dignon reminds him. "And that I had to make it right."

"Do you really think I *fell* down those stairs, Dignon? Do you really think it's a mistake that Willie found me?"

Flashes of him tumbling down the stairs in their old

home blink in his mind, the old man's body slapping the stairs on the way down then landing at the bottom, limbs and head twisted. He has always suspected. Now he knows.

"Willie pushed you."

His father nods wearily.

"Good."

"You still don't get it, do you? You have to make it right."

"I don't have to make anything right," Dignon tells him. "You do."

"I can't," he says. "Only you can."

"I'm supposed to forgive you, is that it? That sets you free?"

His father bows his head, closes his eyes.

"What sets *me* free? Answer that, you fuck. What sets Willie free?"

"It's facing the truth that's hard. That's where the danger is." He raises his head, glances at the television then shifts his eyes to Dignon. "Forgiveness is a gift. This is something else. This is punishment...mine, and yours. Experiencing someone else's pain, the pain you inflicted on them, is the greatest punishment of all. Having to relive it again and again for all eternity, to feel what they felt, to know what they knew, to hurt like they hurt, to experience it endlessly, to live what they live...or would have lived...and to never be able to escape any of it. Not ever, do you understand? Not ever. Don't you see that's what this is? It's what it's always been."

Dignon backs away, into the shadows. Reaching behind him, he feels the rough wall against his palms. "You're a liar."

"Running is easy. It's truth that's hard."

He looks to the window he crawled through, sees the little boy's face peering down at them. Next to him is the man in the smoking jacket, grinning.

Tell me Dignon, where do you think people like me go when they die?

His father thrashes about violently. The wire only cuts deeper.

"Let me out," Dignon says, his back to the cement wall as he slides through the shadows in search of a door. "Let me out!"

The man in the smoking jacket turns away and the little boy replaces the window, pushes the pane back into the frame until it snaps into place. He watches a while longer, expressionless as Dignon's screams grow louder and more frantic.

And then he moves away.

THIRTEEN

The crawlspace...that god-awful tomb...he and Willie packed into it like fish in a tin, struggling to get out and praying for release. *Can't move. Can't breathe. Help us. Please, someone get us out.* Stale air, spider webs, rough cement, dirt and glimpses through the filthy narrow window to the world outside, in light or darkness, freedom so close yet never within reach, dangled there cruelly.

And screams. Always the screams.

Free. No, not free. Loose. There's a difference, isn't there?

Sitting on the toilet, Wilma stands over him, attending to him like a nursemaid, a washcloth in her hand moving across his face and neck, cleaning the blood away. "Hush now," she says. "Stop fidgeting." With surprising composure she finishes wiping the remnants of Barry's blood from Dignon's face then turns her attention to scrubbing it out of his shirt. Once completed, she tosses the washcloth into the sink. It hits the porcelain with a splat and she runs the water until the blood escapes down the drain in a swirl of crimson. "The

Blood In Electric Blue

police," she says in monotone. "The...police."

"Yes," Dignon answers, more cognizant of his surroundings with each passing second. "Sooner or later someone will call the police, won't they Willie? *Won't they?*"

Wilma nods. All the muscles in her face tighten.

Somewhere, Dignon thinks, angels look down upon humanity, watch over and guide people with the promise of something better, protection, deliverance and renewal from all the evil that haunts and so tirelessly pursues them. But not here, he thinks. Not here.

"I have to go," Dignon says.

"I know."

He stands, takes Wilma's chin in his hand and slowly raises her head until their eyes meet. With his other hand he carefully straightens his sister's wig and slides the renegade strands from her eyes. "Everything's going to be fine."

"Of course it will, love," she says halfheartedly.

Somehow, Dignon manages a smile. "You're beautiful. Never forget that. Always remember, Willie. Always, OK?"

Teary-eyed, Wilma whispers, "Always."

* * *

Yellow police tape twists and flutters in the breeze along Borges Lane, the only reminder of Kyle's death jump. Once secured between nearby telephone poles, it has since fallen free and lies in the snow, one end captured by the wind. Dignon watches a while, notices its grace of motion and how its vivid color contrasts with the otherwise white backdrop. There is something terribly lonely about this, he thinks. Not the act of studying an inanimate object on a deserted icy street, rather the object itself, left behind at the mercy of the elements to dance on demand, its existence no longer relevant or akin to its original purpose.

But the wind, he now knows, is not innocent. Not this wind. This wind has brought him here. *She* has brought him here. He pictures Bree waiting in her apartment, knowing it's only a matter of time before he'll succumb and arrive, a subservient puppy summoned to her feet.

This book belongs to Bree Harper.

Obediently, Dignon approaches the building, follows the icy pavement to the front door and hits the appropriate buzzer.

*   *   *

She answers her door dressed in an oversized black and red fleck sweater, tight black slacks and heavy gray socks. Out of shoes he is struck by how short she is. In heels the height difference between them is negligible, an inch or two at most, but now it's at least double that. This is the worst he's ever seen her, hair mussed, eyes bloodshot, nose running and nostrils red, face pale and void of even the light makeup she'd worn previously. One hand clutches the shredded remains of a used tissue, the other the box from which it came. Still, when their eyes lock, Dignon feels his knees weaken and his stomach clench, rapt as ever by her beauty.

"Dignon," she says helplessly, throwing her arms around him. "Kyle, he…"

"I heard. I'm sorry." With a rigid posture, one hand slowly rises to find the small of her back. Her arms tighten around his neck and his palm barely makes contact with her, brushing her sweater. Warmth spreads through his body, along the tops of his shoulders, across

Blood In Electric Blue

his chest and back, down along his stomach and into his groin. She smells wonderful, scrubbed and fresh and powdered and clean, with just a hint of cologne thrown in for good measure. She is everything he's ever imagined feminine beauty and allure to be, and for a moment, Dignon's eyes roll back into his head, his mouth falls open and his bottom lip quivers as he embraces the glow passing from one mythical being to another.

But then she releases him and the electricity is gone. She flashes a look of confusion. "Was it on the news already?"

"A friend of mine was in the neighborhood when the police were here and she told me."

"Come in." She steps away from the door so he can enter then closes it behind him, dabs at her nose with the tissue and motions to the couch. "Can I get you anything, coffee, tea maybe?"

"No, I'm fine. Thanks." He sits on the couch. Something heavy presses against his outer thigh and he realizes the hammer is still in his coat pocket. His palms begin to sweat.

Barry's bruised and bloody face appears in his mind then vanishes in a blink.

"Can I take your coat?" Bree points at it like he's forgotten he still has it on.

"No, that's OK."

"But wouldn't you rather—"

"I'm still a little cold, it's freezing out there." His mind races for an explanation she might accept. "Besides, I can't stay long. I just wanted to check on you."

"You're such a sweetheart." Bree sits next to him, curling one leg beneath her and leaving the other on the floor while words fall from her mouth, escaping in a single rush and tumbling free in a frantic stream as if

186

she's only been allocated a certain amount of time to get them all out. "I can't believe he did it. I never dreamed in a million years Kyle would do something like this. He had quite a temper, as you well know, but suicide? I just—I still can't believe it in any real sense. And to do it right here on this street, I mean—my God—why would he do that other than to hurt me? I know that sounds horribly self-centered considering what's happened but he was obviously making a statement by doing it here and I—we dated for a while it—we were never even that serious, at least I didn't think we were, I didn't—I had no idea things would ever come to this. Kyle obviously had serious issues so I know I shouldn't feel guilty but I do. Maybe if I'd talked to him again I could've prevented this but I was so angry with him, I..." She finally takes a breath, tosses the hideous tissue onto the coffee table and plucks a fresh one from the box. "It's so awful. I just *cannot* believe it."

"Sometimes I wonder if we're in control of any of it," Dignon says, "or if we're just kids strapped into an amusement park ride with no idea where it leads next. All I know is that life doesn't make much sense. And death makes even less."

Bree seems surprised by his comment, like she'd expected a response more simplistic or accommodating. "It certainly seems that way much of the time, doesn't it? Life is often unnecessarily cruel."

"Maybe cruelty is a necessary evil."

"Do you really think there is such a thing?"

Dignon shrugs.

When he offers nothing more she smiles and says, "I'm glad you came, Dignon. To tell you the truth I was going to call you anyway. I didn't...I don't...want to be alone today."

The book is on the table nearby. He glances at it.

Blood In Electric Blue

"We're the same in some ways," Dignon tells her. "We're both alone a lot."

Bree nods sadly, stares down at the cushions beneath her.

"For me it's no wonder. But you…"

"Why is it so hard to imagine I could be lonely too?"

"What happened to Kyle?" he asks abruptly, his tone shifting. "Something must've happened to leave him no choice but to throw himself off a roof."

She delicately scratches the side of her nose with the tip of a fingernail. Despite her magnetism, she is clearly weakened. But is it genuine sorrow and shock, or something else? He can only wonder if doing what she does—luring men to their death through whatever ancient and deadly means her kind harbor—takes something out of her prior to making her more powerful and deadly. "I had no idea he was so desperate," she says. "If I thought for a moment he was capable of taking his own life I would've done something, or at least tried. He never gave any indication he was contemplating such a thing."

"At least it's over now…for him."

Bree raises her head, an earnest look on her face. "I feel so close to you, but I'm not exactly sure why. I'm drawn to you for some reason. I feel this comfort with you it usually takes me months to feel with someone—if ever—and yet I feel it with you more strongly than I ever have with anyone else. And we've only known each other a few days."

"Fate, like you said."

"Must be."

Dignon closes his eyes and gently shifts his position. The bloody hammer in his coat pocket shifts as well, the weight again reminding him of its presence and lethal purpose. The throbbing in his fingertip suddenly becomes worse, sending shooting pains up through his knuckles and into his hand. He rubs it with his other hand until the pain returns to his fingertip, pulsing there like a ticking clock counting the seconds to an imminent event of great significance.

She says nothing, moving instead with such stealth and grace that he doesn't realize Bree has come for him until her palm is pressed delicately against his cheek. Her other arm slides across the back of his shoulders, pulling him closer until their faces touch, and he can feel her breath against his face, mingling with his own as her hair brushes against him.

Dignon wants to fight this—her—but is powerless to do so.

Somewhere very far away, he hears screams.

As her lips touch his chin then cheek and she leans into him, her breasts crush against the side of his arm. He trembles, feels his hands rise from the couch to hold her, as if controlled by someone else. Inhaling traces of her cologne, he lets her lips smother his. Her tongue slides into his mouth, gliding slowly and seductively, warm and moist against his own.

He cannot open his eyes, and yet he sees.

He sees it all.

The road is bumpy and uneven. The car jerks about, rattles as it makes its way along the lonely country road to the cemetery. The old wrought iron gates read: EVERGREEN. *But on this day the grass is dead and brown, the earth cold and frozen, the normally beautiful trees along the edge of the property bare and menacing, reminding him of a cartoon he'd seen where frightening black trees came to life and chased a young boy through a field. As Dignon watches the seemingly endless rows of headstones pass by the window, his breath forming small patches of fog along the glass, he wonders if these trees come to life as well. Perhaps after dark, he thinks.*

Blood In Electric Blue

Once they've parked in the appropriate lane their father shuts off the engine and orders his sons from the car. They do as they're told and follow him to the graveside. His mother's name — Amelia — is carved into the stone along with her date of birth and date of death. Dignon knows the latter date all too well.

His birthday. Today. He is seven years old today. She is seven years dead.

"Say you're sorry," his father growls.

"I'm sorry."

The slap to the back of his head is fast and vicious. It sends Dignon stumbling forward and to his knees, just inches from the stone. He steadies himself and blinks rapidly in an attempt to ward off the stinging pain and dizziness spinning across his vision. Six feet below his knees are the remains of his mother, sealed away in a box. His stomach clenches and he pictures the photograph of her in the living room of their home, the only picture of her he has ever seen.

"Say it like you mean it," his father orders. "Tell your mama you're sorry."

"I'm sorry," Dignon says, fighting away the tears that always come when they do this. "I'm sorry, mama."

Willie goes to him and helps him back to his feet without uttering a word.

"Useless bastard," his father says. "If it wasn't for your miserable ass she'd still be alive. You killed her. Say it."

"I killed her."

"She died right about this time." He considers his watch then glares at Dignon. "We're gonna have one hell of a birthday party today, boy, just like always. We've got to celebrate, right?"

"Yes sir," Dignon answers quietly.

"Get in the car." He glares at Willie. "You too, you little faggot."

Greg F. Gifune

His parka is off and in a heap on the couch behind him. Bree climbs atop him now, straddling his lap then sitting back on her heels, still locked in a deep kiss, her hands holding either side of Dignon's face as they both breathe rapidly, excitedly. His arms move up her back, between her shoulder blades and pull her closer. Her crotch rubs against his and he feels himself harden and strain against his jeans.

Stop, he thinks. *Stop her.*

But he can't. She has him. Bree has him and he cannot stop. He only wants to lose himself in her all the more, to continue to feel and taste and smell her until he can no longer stand it.

The cellar…it's all so vivid: the chair, his father's belt draped across the back of it, the large silver metal buckle dangling there. Beneath it a candle burns, its flame slowly turning the metal red hot while he and Willie sit nude on the cement floor, their backs to the wall, watching their father pace near the cellar door, drinking and mumbling and ranting as he always does before they begin.

The belt is for Dignon. The chair is for Willie.

When their father throws the booze aside and takes up the bottle of perfume from the shelf on the far wall, waving it around and explaining as he does every time that it was the same brand their mother wore, Dignon and Willie know the horror is underway. There will be no turning back now. Like always, there will be no way out or even a means by which to forget. It – this – will never go away. He will brand it into their souls, burn it deep like the scar it is.

He snatches Willie first, grabs him by the wrist and yanks him to his feet. Laughing, he pours the perfume over Willie's head until the boy is soaked. Reeking, Willie collapses next to the chair, choking and gagging.

Dignon offers no assistance. He learned long ago that the

Blood In Electric Blue

punishment for such digressions is far worse than what is already planned for them. To question or fight back only makes things worse. Besides, he and Willie both know that one day their father will probably kill them anyway, that one day he will not be able to stop and they will die here in this horrible old cellar.

Their father puts the empty perfume down and pulls the belt from the back of the chair. The buckle glows orange for a second or two then the metal shifts to an odd darker hue.

As Willie climbs up onto the chair, kneels forward and hangs his upper body across the back of it in place of the belt, his face just inches from the still-burning candle, Dignon stands and faces the wall. Bracing himself for the pain to come, he knows the only saving grace is he will be unconscious by the time his father finishes with him and returns his attention to his brother.

He feels his sweater coming off, sliding up over his belly and chest, snagging on his head and then falling free. But still, Dignon does not open his eyes. Not even when the fear of being nude from the waist up occurs to him, the horror of being seen as he sees himself, ugly and bloated and weak. Through a veil of embarrassment he thinks: How hideous I must look, how grotesque. She must be sickened and stunned by this awful blob sitting before her.

Yet Bree says nothing. Instead her hands are all over him, touching and squeezing and stroking as pleasure gushes through him, momentarily canceling out the self-conscious nervousness. Between kisses, a soft moan escapes his lips.

"Come with me to the bedroom, Dignon," she whispers in his ear. Climbing off him, she takes his hand. "Now, come with me now."

He turns toward the bedroom, and in doing so,

reveals his bare back to her.

A palpable change in the air stops him where he sits. The excited rhythm of Bree's breathing ceases with a sharp and sudden intake, an audible gasp.

"*Oh my God*," she says, whispering again.

Dignon opens his eyes and sits back against the couch. "Sorry, I..." He grabs his sweater and quickly drapes it over his chest. He's saved. "I know it's horrible to look at, I'm horrible to look at, I—"

"No, don't, I—*I'm* sorry, I didn't know, I..." Bree's trembling hands find either side of her face. "Your back, you...did your *father* do that to you?"

He nods. He knows what it looks like, though he hasn't seen it himself in years. It requires he stand with his back to a mirror then turn and crane his neck behind him, only to gaze upon a network of thick scars slashed and whipped into his flesh, the raised white tissue like swollen veins crisscrossing his torso. Dignon pulls the sweater back on and stares at the floor.

Bree touches his hand. "How could he do such a thing?"

"He did as bad and sometimes worse to Willie."

"But why?" She blinks free a tear that rolls slowly along her cheek.

"Because our mother was the only person he ever really loved. Because he hated me for killing her the day I was born. Because Willie and I were there instead of her, in place of her, and he didn't want us. We were just all that was left behind."

"He was a monster."

"Yes," Dignon says. "He was."

So am I. And so are you.

Her hand still touching his, she rubs her thumb slowly back and forth against his skin. "I'll never under-stand this life," she says quietly. "Even when I get

Blood In Electric Blue

glimpses of understanding, clues as to what life is or what it's really all about, none of it ever seems to last long enough for me to fully comprehend it."

Dignon looks directly into her beautiful eyes, burrows deeper until he reaches a place far from this apartment and the horrible memories nesting in his mind, a profound and cavernous part of Bree Harper's soul where her own personal piece of eternity resides.

This time it is Dignon's gaze that captivates her.

When he speaks, he does so slowly, thoughtfully. "It's like at night, when it's raining and there's cars and headlights moving through the darkness, through the window. Everything's shiny and wet and looks so new. Undamaged, you know? Alive. Everything looks alive. And just for a moment, the whole world makes sense, it all fits together. You know it. You see it so clearly. And then it's gone."

Bree sighs, runs her hands seductively up along her sides and onto her breasts, then flops back against the couch cushions as if overcome. "Let's go to the bedroom, Dignon."

"I know what you are," he says, the tightness in his crotch receding.

She snaps out of her trance but offers no response.

"Kyle knew what you are," Dignon continues. "He knew before he died, before you lured him to his death."

"Lured him? What are you saying?"

"But you can't have me. You can't destroy me."

Her eyes narrow into a squint. "Why would I want to destroy you?"

"You can't trap me because I can resist you." He smiles as his strength and resolve, his clarity of mind, returns. "My pain makes it possible. The beauty of it gives me the strength to fight you."

"There is no beauty in pain, Dignon, only sorrow."

Greg F. Gifune

He straightens his sweater, smoothes it down over his belly. "You don't have to lie to me Bree, not to me."

"OK look, I don't know who it is you think I am, but I'm just a simple person with a life and a job, with dreams and disappointments like everyone else."

"Kyle looked into you before he died, he—"

"Kyle was apparently quite ill. He threw himself off a roof."

"You didn't check out, that's what he said."

"*Check out*? What does that even mean? What are you talking about?"

Dignon casually slides a hand across the couch toward his parka. "You're not who you claim to be, who you pretend to be. I know the truth."

Bree's expression changes from confusion to fear. She inches away from him then stands and nervously straightens her hair. "I've obviously made a mistake, I—I think I'd like you to leave."

"Why would you want me to leave?" he asks, sliding a hand into his coat pocket. "You've worked so hard to draw me here."

"I don't know what the hell you're talking about." She moves toward the door, manically straightening her hair and clothing as if to obliterate any trace of him.

Rather than follow her to the door, Dignon remains where he is and waits to see if she will show her true form or continue to retreat and play her mind games.

"Truly," she says, hugging her shoulders, "I'd appreciate it if you'd leave, all right? You're making me extremely uncomfortable."

"And why is that?" His fingers find the hammer, close slowly over the handle. It is still sticky with Barry's blood, but he now knows if he needs to, he can use it to defend himself with extreme prejudice. "Because I can resist you, and sirens can't survive resistance, can they

Blood In Electric Blue

Bree?"

She shakes her head. "What is it with the men in this town? Are you all insane? Sirens? Like in mythology? You can't be serious."

"We don't have to pretend anymore. I wish you could see the beauty in that like I can. I wish you could feel it too."

"All I've done is tried to be your friend."

The Death Maker carries a curse from its ancestors, usually those of a parent.

"No. You want to enslave me."

They are often sought after, enslaved or destroyed by a myriad of evil beings or practitioners of black magic...

"You want to destroy me."

...who seek to draw power by possessing the darkness engulfing a Death Maker's soul.

"What is wrong with you?" Bree asks. "Where did you get these ideas?"

"Exactly where you wanted me to," he says, motioning to the coffee table and the copy of *Mythical Beings in a Mortal World* that resides there.

She laughs, but it's nervous laughter, frightened laughter. "For God's sake, it's just a book, a—"

"I know what I am, Bree. And I know what you are."

Sirens are immortal...

"All those cities, all those towns you've lived in over the years, the decades, the centuries. How many Kyles have there been? How many bodies and souls are floating in your wake? And a Death Maker like me can only make you stronger and even more powerful, able to cause more pain, death and destruction."

...except for those rare occasions when a man fails to fall under their spell.

Bree's eyes bounce from one wall to the other as she leans back against the door and reaches blindly for the knob.

When this happens, a siren will throw herself into the sea as a means of escape…

"I know you'll run," Dignon says, slowly rising to his feet. "And I know where you'll run to."

…but will instantly be transformed to stone.

"Please don't do this," she says, tears welling in her eyes. "Whatever I've done, whatever you think I've done, I—I'm sorry, I…I just want to live my life as best I can, like everyone else."

"But you're not like everyone else. And neither am I."

"You're a deeply wounded person, Dignon. What your father did to you, what he's still doing to you even now, it breaks my heart, but I—please don't hurt me."

"Hurt you?" Dignon holds tight to the hammer but leaves it in his pocket. "I won't hurt you. You'll hurt yourself. You have no choice."

"We always have a choice, Dignon. All of us."

"I reject you. You can't make me fall under your spell like the others, and that means your number is up, Bree. It's over. In a very short while, we'll both be free. Forever."

She yanks open the apartment door and runs into the hallway, screaming for help. Calling for neighbors to phone the police, she bangs on several doors then dashes for the stairs.

Calmly, Dignon follows. There is no reason to chase after her.

He knows exactly where she's going.

*   *   *

The cold no longer bothers him. Like his demons, it's still there but no match for his newfound strength. He

Blood In Electric Blue

moves with a purposeful stride out the front door of the apartment building. Surely the ruckus Bree caused has resulted in several tenants phoning the police, so there's not much time. She's nowhere in sight, but has left behind tracks in the snow. He follows her exact route, slipping around the side of the building then up and over a large snowdrift that leads to an incline and the beach below.

Out of breath, Dignon staggers down across the snowy beach, nearly losing his footing. The sea is choppy and ominous, the wind stronger here.

But for the motion of waves, everything is still and frozen.

He stops a moment, scans the area.

The black sweater gives her away. At a full run, she has a good fifty yards on him, and with a quick glance back over her shoulder, she stumbles up onto a long but narrow stone jetty that juts out into the sea. Though the large stones are mostly dark in color, the snow and ice covers great portions of them, allowing for only occasional pieces of stone to show through. At a distance it looks like a shelf of ice and snow has frozen atop the ocean itself.

"A siren will throw itself into the sea as a means of escape," he mumbles, breaking into a run himself. Of all the places Bree Harper could've gone, why here? Why run to water unless she has no choice? Dignon pulls the hammer from his coat pocket as he runs. If she tries to take him with her he'll be ready, but he has to be there to see her demise, he has to be sure.

By the time he reaches the jetty his eyes are watering from the cold, he can barely breathe and is experiencing the beginnings of chest pains. Forty or so yards ahead of him, Bree has run out of jetty.

Dignon steps up onto the first stone and once he has

198

good footing, moves carefully along the jetty. The wind whips ocean water up into his face in a spray of little icy needles, but he presses on until he's within thirty feet of her.

"Wait!" she says, frantically looking around from a crouched position, her hands raised.

She no longer looks quite so beautiful, Dignon thinks. More like a cornered animal, a predator not used to being the prey and unprepared for the fight.

"Dignon, wait!" she screams, pushing her hands out farther in front of her for emphasis. "Stop—please, I—I'll do anything you want! Anything, Dignon, anything you say! Just stop!"

He feels a smile crease his face. "Don't try to tempt me. It won't work."

Her cheeks, flushed bright red from the cold, are stained with tears. "Please," she says again, eyes attempting a seductive stare. "Anything, OK? Just tell me what you want."

"I want it to stop." His smile fades. "I want the pain to stop, the...the nightmares."

"I haven't caused your pain, Dignon, and I'm not a part of your nightmares, it's not me, you've made me a part of them but I—I want to help you, will you—will you let me help you?"

Somewhere in the distance comes an odd sound. He thinks it might be the wind but can't be sure. It almost sounds human, like someone calling or shouting from far off. A trick, he decides, an attempt to distract him. She is a crafty and calculating creature and he must not allow her to fool him.

He takes another step toward her and something slams into his back. The impact is similar to someone punching him from behind and hits him with such force it causes him to stumble forward. As he turns to see what's happened, a second impact slams into him, and this time as he staggers, the hammer drops from his grasp, bounces off the rocks and is swallowed by waves crashing the jetty. Instinctually, Dignon arches his back and reaches behind him to the areas hit. Bree screams and a third blow lands.

Dignon tries to stay upright, but now feels pain burning through him.

He tumbles face-first onto the jetty, just inches from Bree's feet.

*   *   *

It is the wind he hears first. But as the darkness lifts enough for his vision to clear, he hears other sounds as well. The slap of ocean against rocks…the crackle of nearby fires…the cries and screams of trapped and dying souls.

Bree appears before him, standing at the very edge of the jetty in all her glory. Her nude body draped in a sheer white flowing gown, her hair high and full, eyes fiery and arms extended out on either side of her like an enormous bird. Her face is a mask of death and pain, and yet, hers is the most alluring and magnificently beautiful face and body he has ever seen, even more intoxicating than before.

Behind her, flames burn atop the surface of the ocean and the voices of those drowning and dying cry out through the darkness amidst debris and the skeletal remains of ships and floating carcasses. Before this panorama of destruction, she is alive as he's never before seen her, feeding off the mayhem and torture to reveal her true nature. Her incredible beauty juxtaposed with such violence and horror, such ugliness, somehow makes her more powerful, as if her beauty itself is born of it, drawn from it, strengthened by it. Her lips part, and a screech explodes from her as she throws back her head and pushes out her chest, breasts wet and slick, nipples taut in the cold.

Once at her feet, the siren's song is no longer captivating or mysterious. It is instead the wail of a wounded animal, the lurid sobs of an addict in need of a fix, the hysterical cries of a child in the throes of a hellish nightmare. It is death.

*   *   *

Up through darkness, sounds of earth and water emerge: the crash of ocean surf and howling winds. And then he feels them too, the spray of saltwater on his face and neck, the cold current of air slicing through him, burrowing to the bone and icing him over like a corpse, some lifeless thing with blood no longer flowing but rather clotted and congealed in the vein. Something once alive yet not quite wholly dead, a frozen embryo still capable of life, of *being* alive, but suspended somewhere just shy of it.

The subtle tingle of pain pulses through his torso as Dignon, still lying on his stomach along the jetty, struggles to look back over his shoulder. In the distance lies the beach, what appear to be several official-looking vehicles and the apartment building beyond. Several figures he cannot quite make out with any specificity move quickly across the sand, and in the distance, gliding up over faraway rooftops, he sees the smokestacks exhaling over the city like dragon breath. An attentive god, omnipresent and omnipotent, it oversees everything in its detached way, an observer of the lost souls wandering about its empire, forever shrouded in mystery and cloaked in questions, the answers riddles and mazes for those who believe, those who notice, those who need to look deeper and see further into what lies behind and beyond the smoke, the sky, the dark and the light.

Something distracts him.

A figure runs toward them, moves along the beginnings of the jetty with impressive balance. Dignon cannot make out much, as his vision is blurred and for some reason unknown to him, continues to come in and out of focus, but he is almost certain even at this distance that he's seen this man before. A man in uniform, running, something in his hand—a gun?—and...is he calling out to them?

Or is it Willie he hears just then, saying something in his ear?

Laughing, she's...she's laughing.

So long ago, when they'd still laughed, on those nights when their father was away and it was just the two of them, free to do as they pleased. Willie would make *Jiffy Pop* popcorn and they'd read their comic books. Dignon would tell stories, or if there was enough time, they'd watch television. Movies and TV shows, events, anything at all. Dr. J playing basketball, bleached-blonde women wrestlers jumping around a ring and screaming at delighted fans, cartoons like Bugs Bunny and Speed Racer, and shows like The Banana Splits.

But it is movies Dignon remembers most of all, all sorts of wonderful movies that could take them away, transport them to different places and times, different lives, different realities. He remembers classics like James Dean in *East of Eden*, Jane Fonda in *Klute*, as well as all the great exploitations flicks Willie and he would watch together. He remembers comedies like *Mother, Jugs and Speed*, a movie about ambulance drivers starring Bill Cosby and Raquel Welch, and how he and Willie had laughed and laughed until the scene toward the end when Bill Cosby's partner is shot and killed by a drug addict. It all comes rushing back, all the memories and flashes, pieces of film cut and spliced together and running through his head.

All they had to do was watch and experience. All they had to do was forget, even if just for a little while.

Just think of a movie. Think of it and go there. Make it your own.

Make it real.

Make them memories, Willie, our memories.

It'll be all right.

Dignon rolls back onto his stomach, gags and coughs, feels something wet and warm drool out over his bottom lip. He cannot feel his legs for some reason.

Bree is crouched at the very edge of the jetty, her face contorted in horror, her hands clutching either side of her head as if to somehow prevent sanity's escape.

"Did I have it wrong?" he asks, gagging a second time. The metallic taste of blood fills his mouth. "Did I have it wrong?"

Bree stares at him through tear-filled eyes but says nothing.

Are we mythical beings in a mortal world, he wonders, *or mortal beings in a mythical world?*

Bree says something but her voice is muffled by the crashing surf.

He watches her stand, legs shaky, her expression suddenly stoic.

And as she takes a tentative step toward him her feet slip out from under her. Mouth open in a silent scream, Bree Harper falls backward into the ocean and is devoured.

The memory of his mother's photograph slips past his mind's eye.

Blood In Electric Blue

Dignon crawls after Bree until he reaches the edge and can look down into the water. Vomiting more blood he pushes farther until he has almost fallen in himself, his face just inches from the sea and reflecting back up at him in the turbulent waves.

The pain in his finger pulses...

Help me, Dig. Help me.

...the raw patch where his skin has scraped off, red and throbbing...

I'm sorry. I'd save you if I could.

The crawlspace...their crypt...he and Willie packed into it so tightly neither can move nor properly breathe. Dead, humid air, spider webs, rough cement—Dignon's finger moving slowly back and forth across a small section of it just to his left, scraping and in constant motion to remind him that he is still able to move even some small part of whatever remains of him, to remind him he is still alive—or something similar—and that there is still hope.

Sooner or later someone will call the police, won't they Willie?

The cold water splashes his face, and as he blinks and coughs out another mouthful of blood, Bree vanishes in the dark ocean and the sea again reflects his face. Tormented and scarred.

Sounds of hurried footsteps coming closer from somewhere behind him...

Who's there?

And in the ocean's mirror: reflections of rotating patterns, blue lights from the beach behind him spin along the surface. Like the blood in my veins, Dignon thinks.

Are we dead Willie?

Blood in electric blue...

Have we died?

Revolving and growing stronger, gliding ghostlike along the walls of the cellar, through the darkness, brighter with each pass…

We're just lost.

Closer, like the voices telling them it will be all right, like the footsteps…

Lost in the dark a while.

Like the blood leaking from his open mouth, red now that it's left him.

Loose. Loose but not free. Never free.

"What is the privilege of the dead?" he hears Nikki ask, quoting her favorite film from some forgotten corner of her apartment. "To die no more."

Below the choppy water, Bree's body sinks in freefall. A body of flesh and blood, a body turned to stone, or simply the residue of myth.

Dignon looks closer, to be sure.

And there, just below the waves, is his answer.

ABOUT THE AUTHOR

Greg F. Gifune's novels, stories and collections have been published in a wide range of magazines and anthologies all over the world, and have recently garnered interest from Hollywood. He is the author of the short story collections *Heretics* and *Down To Sleep*, and the novels *Deep Night*, *The Bleeding Season*, *Saying Uncle*, *A View From the Lake*, *Dominion*, *Night Work*, and *Drago Descending*. Also a freelance editor and Associate Editor at Delirium Books, Greg lives in Massachusetts with his wife Carol and a bevy of very cool kitties. He can be reached online through his official web site at: www.gregfgifune.com.

CPSIA information can be obtained at www.ICGtesting.com
Printed in the USA
BVOW031105220212

283524BV00006B/139/P